IELTS

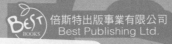
倍斯特出版事業有限公司
Best Publishing Ltd.

一次就考到

雅思單字

掌握最新出題資訊且總是切中核心要點

韋爾 ◎ 著

7+

MP3

三大學習特色 精選「循環」必考字彙／精練「中階」同義轉換能力／厚實「高分」字彙運用能力

掌握最新歷屆試題字彙：收錄《劍12》-《劍14》官方核心字彙，了解最新出題趨勢和變化，以最佳狀態迎戰考試。

提升推測文意的能力：藉由試題演練**強化「臆測」**近義詞的能力，有效增進閱讀和聽力臨場答題反應力。

強化英文寫作實力：背誦佳句並將高階字彙運用在雅思寫作中，**優化「字詞」**使用能力，一舉獲取寫作佳績。

EDITOR 作者序

　　在英語學習道路上，單字一直都是學習的基石，在備考上的重要性是不容小覷的。考生仍需要一定的字彙量來應戰雅思測驗中所包含的四個單項，我一直認為「是否有符合考生需求」這點才是最重要的。但是就準備單字來說，書店單字書琳瑯滿目，各有特色和賣點，有些書籍精心編排和設計，但是包含太多冷澀的字彙。有些難度過高，在英語報章雜誌中甚至不會出現；也有些書籍中編列的字彙過於簡易，等同仍未協助到學習和實質的得分。而直接去寫劍橋雅思官方試題又覺得太難，會需要背誦一定程度的字彙之後再來寫劍橋雅思官方試題。

　　考生在這樣的過渡期時，就會需要一本難度適中且字彙是精選過、確定會在雅思閱讀考試等主題中常出現的單字書。因此，我在撰寫這本雅思單字書不斷地在思考這個問題，最後由《劍橋雅思 12-14》的閱讀測驗中精選單字，並規劃成 36 個

單元，每個單字均附例句和錄音，協助考生更充分有效的備考。從《劍橋雅思 12-14》中精選字彙的主因是：《劍橋雅思 12-14》最近三本官方公佈的試題，除了份量適中也反映了最新的題型變化。另外一方面的考量，是這些字彙會在同類型的閱讀篇章中不斷出現，所以藉由背誦這些字等同做了最佳的準備。例如一篇生物類的文章出現的相關字，可能與其他官方試題或考場中遇到的生物類試題，有重疊性高的主要字彙，而這些字彙是背誦的目標，因為它們會循環出現。

另外，書籍中還規劃了「Vocabulary in Context」的實戰演練，考生可以藉由這個單元練習更多的同義字的表達並累積信心。選擇題式的設計和選出粗體字的同義字，是演練同義字且又不會造成太多挫折感的規劃，這也是掌握初階同義轉換在四個單項中最基礎的部分，所以從這個部分切入來做學習會是最合適的。相信考生在演練這些試題後，能從獨立撰寫「一篇

單篇」官方閱讀試題到「一整回三篇」官方試題，大幅提升實力。考生可以將其他在《劍橋雅思官方試題》中遇到的重要字彙列在自己的筆記本中複習，時間夠充分可以一直往前寫，若時間不太夠用就寫最接近的幾回測驗即可，更前面的試題可能太舊了。

　　你不見得需要準備一萬字以上的字彙量才能考取高分（當然能背更多單字，對於提升個人英語水平而言是好的），但是用最短時間考取高分的考生，他們不一定花了許多時間背一堆單字，而是掌握了循環字彙和答題技巧。有些專業字和學術字彙，搭配同位語的學習和掌握循環字彙就能迅速考到高分（同位語一定是由更簡易的單字組成來解釋這個專有名詞，所以由簡易名詞片語理解這個字就可以了，確實不需要背）。畢竟，看一篇英文文章後在筆記本中列了許多單字確實會增加挫折感。對考生來說最重要的部分是掌握這些「循環字彙」再開始

寫官方閱讀或聽力試題，如此也能增進信心。最後祝福所有考

生都能獲取理想成績。

韋爾 敬上

INSTRUCTIONS
使用說明

Unit 22 《劍 13》
Test 4 Reading Passage 1

Cutty Sark: the Fastest Sailing Ship of all Time
卡提沙克號：史上最快的帆船

KEY 253 ▶ MP3 22
-- vessel /ˈvɛsəl/ *n.* 船隻；容器、器皿；血管、導管
• Vessels are sailing at an exceedingly great speed so that fishermen can catch up with the last harvest.
船隻正以極快的速度行駛，這樣一來漁夫們就能捕獲最後一次的捕撈。

KEY 254
-- dominate /ˈdɑmən,et/ *vt. vi.* 支配、占優勢
• Even though crocodiles are dominating the swamp and nearby river, pythons do pose a great threat to them.
即使鱷魚在沼澤和鄰近的溪邊佔優勢，巨蟒對牠們造成很大程度的威脅。

KEY 255
-- laden /ˈledən/ *adj.* 充滿的、負載的、苦惱的

KEY 256
-- misfortune /mɪsˈfɔrtʃən/ *n.* 不幸、災禍、壞運氣
• The misfortune of the crocodile is to get targeted by an agile cheetah.
鱷魚的不幸是被靈巧的獵豹鎖定目標。

KEY 257
-- daunting /ˈdɔntɪŋ/ *adj.* 使人畏縮的
• The daunting task is designed to frighten most newly recruits.
令人畏縮的任務是設計用來嚇唬大多數的新聘員工。

KEY 258
-- succeed /səkˈsid/ *vi.* 成功、繼續、繼承；*vt.* 繼...之後、接著...發生
• The young prince succeeded the throne and inherited an enormous amount of wealth.
年輕王子繼承了王位而且繼承了巨大的財富。

KEY 259
-- replacement /rɪplˈesmənt/ *n.* 替換、代替；代替的人

• The colossal ship is laden with gold and silver, making it a target for pirates.
巨型船艦裝載黃金和銀，讓它成了海盜的目標。

106

107

精選雅思循環必考字彙

掌握《劍 12》-《劍 14》其實就夠了

要在短時間內完成備考，你要懂得取巧喔！

由書中內容優化四個單項的準備時間，智勝考試

● 提供給考生最新資訊，消除考生所有疑慮，從
劍橋雅思出題回推，時間絕對花在刀口上，記
憶跨主題會出現的字彙，掌握書中字彙就能巧
取高分。

• KEY 283

-- entirety /ɪntˈaɪətɪ/ *n.* 全面、全部、全體、完全

• The entirety of the strawberries in the warehouse was stolen by experienced employees who are desperate for money.

在倉庫裡頭全部的草莓都被急切用錢的有經員工給偷走了。

• KEY 284

-- unforgeable /ˌʌnfˈɔrdʒ əbl/ *adj.* 不可鍛造的

• The broken sword is unforgeable unless the temperature reaches at least 3,000 Celsius.

斷裂的劍是不可鍛造的，除非溫度達到至少攝氏 3000 度。

• KEY 285

-- pleasurable /plˈɛʒəbəl/ *adj.* 快樂的、愉快的、心情舒暢的

• After consuming ten giant mantises, the female chameleon feels pleasurable and maintains quite friendly towards other male chameleons.

在食用 10 隻大型螳螂後，雌性變色龍感到心情舒暢，對於其他雄性變色龍維持相當友好的態度。

• KEY 286

-- sensation /sɛnsˈeʃən/ *n.* 感覺、感情、感動

• The female tiger has a strange sensation towards the latest arrival.

雌性老虎對於新來的訪客有著奇怪的感覺。

• KEY 287

-- displeasure /dɪsplˈɛʒə/ *n.* 不快、不滿、生氣

• The appearance of chameleons turning red can be the demonstration of their displeasure.

變色龍的外表轉變成紅色可能是在展示牠們的不快。

• KEY 288

-- desirable /dɪzˈaɪrabəl/ *adj.* 稱心的、中意的、理想的、希望的

• The male impala has found a desirable mate, but is get tested by her.

黑斑羚已經找到中意的伴侶，但卻要接受她的考驗。

包含各主題，拓展口說和寫作思路

背誦例句，同步強化表達和提高四個單項的分數

● 由例句強化各種句型表達，強化寫作 variety
並豐富化表達語彙，也能將各主題的話題應用
在口說和寫作各情境，不辭窮應戰口說和寫作
考試，同步獲取七分以上成績。

有效建立閱讀內文和試題的連結

累積數百個同義字

強化「對應同義考點」能力

順暢化答題時間，在時限內完成試題

● 雅思主題的隨機搭配和出題確實常讓許多考生頭痛，有些時候遇到更不擅長的主題時，更容易因為答題不順暢感而造成無法於時間內完成試題的窘境。藉由書中規劃的試題演練能夠迅速建立數百個同義字並改善答題不順暢感，畢竟「對應」到同義考點等同於能迅速答題且答好。抓住這點並持續寫官方試題就能降低備考時的難度且達到理想成績。

⑰ Three lions are trying to **exhaust** the strength of a small elephant.
exhaust is in the closest meaning to this word.
A. consume   B. insinuate
C. exhort   D. mitigate

⑱ The **definitive** moment for an ostrich's life depends on the kick to the abdomen of the cheetah.
definitive is in the closest meaning to this word.
A. clandestine   B. defining
C. incongruous   D. raucous

⑲ The male ostrich ultimately **exceeds** his rival winning the heart of the female ostrich.
exceeds is in the closest meaning to this word.
A. chides   B. surpasses
C. synchronizes   D. insinuates

⑳ Zebras are known for their **distinctive** stripes, whereas giraffes are noted for their long necks.
distinctive is in the closest meaning to this word.
A. tenacious   B. peculiar
C. robust   D. vociferous

⑰ 三頭獅子正試圖耗盡小象的力氣。
exhaust 的意思最接近於這個字。
A. 耗盡   B. 暗指
C. 規勸   D. 減輕

⑱ 鴕鳥性命的決定性的時刻仰賴於踢到獵豹腹部的一擊。
definitive 的意思最接近於這個字。
A. 神秘的   B. 決定性的
C. 不一致的   D. 喧鬧的

⑲ 雄性鴕鳥最終超過了他的敵手贏得雌性鴕鳥的芳心。
exceeds 的意思最接近於這個字。
A. 嘲笑   B. 優於
C. 使同步   D. 暗指

⑳ 斑馬以牠們具特色的斑紋而聞名，而長頸鹿以牠們的長脖子為人所知。
distinctive 的意思最接近於這個字。
A. 堅韌的   B. 獨特的
C. 健壯的   D. 喧嚷的

答案 ⑰ A　⑱ B　⑲ B　⑳ B

超強附錄

重新複習常見的高階字

趁這次一併將這些全部都記起來吧！

● 除了寫試題跟對完答案外，更重要的一點
是也把選項相關的單字一併記下，試題中
的選項均為課堂和書籍中，考生常查找的
單字，而又特別容易又在一段時間後忘記
的，趁這次一起把這些都記起來吧，順便
提升字彙的能力。

雅思單字　附錄

精選高階字彙

placid *adj.* 寧靜的；平和的	**regression** *n.* 退化；復原
presumptuous *adj.* 放肆的；冒昧的	**vicarious** *adj.* 感同身受的
clairvoyance *n.* 洞察力	**inane** *adj.* 空虛的；愚蠢的
dissipate *v.* 使消散；揮霍	**irrevocable** *adj.* 不可挽回的
innuendo *n.* 諷刺	**reprehensible** *adj.* 應該指責的
insidious *adj.* 陰險的；狡詐的	**relegate** *v.* 貶謫；放逐
opportune *adj.* 怡好的，適宜的	**attrition** *n.* 損耗；磨損
solicitous *adj.* 熱心的；熱切期望的	**ostracize** *v.* 放逐；排斥
emolument *n.* 薪水；津貼；酬金	**contingency** *n.* 偶然事件；可能性
recondite *adj.* 深奧的；默默無聞	**liaison** *n.* 聯繫；私通
nonchalant *adj.* 冷靜的	**reinstate** *v.* 使恢復；使復職
hubbub *n.* 吵鬧聲；騷動	**inundate** *v.* 充滿；壓倒
unassuming *adj.* 不裝腔作勢的	**circumvent** *v.* 以智取勝
flamboyant *adj.* 浮誇的；炫耀的	**disseminate** *v.* 散播；宣傳
prognosis *n.* 預知	**raucous** *adj.* 刺耳的；喧鬧的
euphoric *adj.* 心情愉快的	**decrement** *n.* 減少、減少量
maudlin *adj.* 感情脆弱的	**vehemently** *adv.* 強烈地；熱烈地
impetuous *adj.* 魯莽的；衝動的	**ostentatious** *adj.* 炫耀的、賣弄的
tentative *adj.* 試驗性的、嘗試的	**ennui** *n.* 倦怠；無聊

318

精選高階字彙

infallible *adj.* 絕對可靠的；絕對有效的	**impassion** *v.* 使激動
inadvertent *adj.* 不注意的；怠慢的	**tantamount** *adj.* 同等的，相當於的
dexterous *adj.* 敏捷的；靈巧的	**contentment** *n.* 滿足、知足；滿意
lethargy *n.* 昏睡、瞌睡；不活潑	**vociferous** *adj.* 喧嚷的
optimum *n.* 最適宜條件；最佳效果	**fortuitous** *adj.* 幸運的；吉祥的
embellish *v.* 美化；裝飾	**coalition** *n.* 結合、聯合
squelch *v.* 把……鎮住；壓制	**discretion** *n.* 謹慎、考慮周到
dormancy *n.* 睡眠、冬眠	**forestall** *v.* 先發制（人）
belligerent *adj.* 好戰的；好鬥的	**insinuate** *v.* 含沙射影地說；暗指
tenuous *adj.* 纖細的、稀薄的	**espouse** *v.* 擁護、支持
despondent *adj.* 沮喪的	**denunciation** *n.* 斥責；譴責；告發
facetious *adj.* 滑稽的；好開玩笑的	**clandestine** *adj.* 祕密的；暗中的
charlatan *adj.* 騙人的	**inexactness** *n.* 不正確；不精密
synchronize *v.* 同時發生	**recourse** *n.* 依靠、依賴
nebulous *adj.* 朦朧的；含糊的	**chide** *v.* 責備；責怪
retribution *n.* 報應；懲罰；報答	**perfunctory** *adj.* 敷衍的、馬虎的
macabre *adj.* 令人毛骨悚然的	**distraught** *adj.* 心煩意亂的
unfavorable *adj.* 不利的、不適宜	**esoteric** *adj.* 深奧的；難理解的
sordid *adj.* 下賤的；利慾薰心的	**grotesque** *adj.* 古怪的；怪誕的

319

目次 CONTENTS

1 Part
雅思精選必考字彙

2 Part
實力檢測 *Vocabulary in Context*

Part 1

雅思精選必考字彙

Part 1 由《劍橋雅思 12-14》的閱讀測驗中精選單字,並規劃成 36 個單元,每個單字均附例句和錄音,修正口說和寫作中句子的表達,並大幅縮短四個單項的備考時間,事半功倍獲取平均 7 以上的成績。

Unit 1 《劍 14》
Test 1 Reading Passage 1

The Importance of Children's play
孩童玩耍的重要性

KEY 1 ▶ MP3 01

-- magical /m'ædʒɪkəl/ *adj.* 魔術的、有魔力的

• The library is designed to be unbelievably **magical**, and the button of entering a study room is on the painting.
這個圖書館的設計是具有無比魔力的,而進入研讀室的開關就在一幅圖畫上。

KEY 2

-- gallant /g'æpənt/ *adj.* 英勇的、壯麗的

• The turn of the actor on the horseback is considered extremely **gallant** by many cinemagoers.
男演員在馬背上的轉身被許多電影愛好者視為是極度英勇的。

KEY 3

-- enchanting /ɛntʃ'æntɪŋ/ *adj.* 迷人的、嫵媚的、迷惑的

• The forest flowers are toxic in a way that makes inhalers

enchanting and hypnotic.

森林花朵是具有毒性的，而這種毒性能夠讓吸入者感到被誘惑且被催眠。

• KEY 4

-- fantasy /fˈæntəsi/ *n.* 幻想、白日夢

- Cindy is an office lady who has the **fantasy** of dating a muscular Australian fireman.

辛蒂是個對與肌肉發達的澳洲消防員約會存有著幻想的上班族。

• KEY 5

-- repercussion / r,ipɚkˈʌʃən / *n.* 彈回、反響、反射

- Swimming in a sizable lake for a few years has a **repercussion** for his success in winning the Olympic champion.

這幾年來在相當大的湖泊裡游泳反映出他能夠成功贏得奧林匹亞的冠軍。

• KEY 6

-- extol /ɪkstˈol/ *v.* 頌揚、稱讚、吹捧

- "Employee of the month" is an award used to **extol** someone who does well in a month and will be given huge bonuses.

「當月最佳雇員」是個用於讚賞在一個月內表現良好者的獎勵，且會給予鉅額獎金。

🔑 KEY 7

-- mindful /m'aındfəl/ *adj.* 深切注意的、留神的、留心的

• The forest has multiple poisonous flowers, so you should be very **mindful**.

這個森林有多樣的毒花,因此你應該要非常注意。

🔑 KEY 8

-- curtail /kə·t'el/ *v.* 縮減、剝奪、簡略

• The company has **curtailed** several benefits, such as dental and children care, due to the economic downturn.

由於經濟蕭條,公司已經縮減了幾項獎勵,例如牙齒和兒童照護。

🔑 KEY 9

-- perception /pə·s'ɛpʃən/ *n.* 知覺、感覺、領悟力

• The wicked witch has keen **perception** and mind reading, so very few people can conceal their thoughts in front of her.

邪惡的女巫有著敏銳的感知能力和讀心術,因此非常少的人能夠在她面前隱匿他們的想法。

🔑 KEY 10

-- unfamiliar /ˌʌnfəm'ɪljə·/ *adj.* 不熟悉的、陌生的、外行的

• Swimming in different oceans always gives Tom an **unfamiliar** feeling, and it somehow makes his skin really tactful.

在不同的海洋中游泳總是給湯姆不熟悉的感覺，而這不知如何的讓他皮膚感知變得非常熟練。

• KEY 11

-- predictor /prɪd'ɪktɚ/ *n.* 預言者、預測因子

• The **predictor** used to gauge the future success of the employees is now considered outdated.

過去用於衡量員工未來成功的預測因子現在已被視為是過時的了。

• KEY 12

-- neurodevelopmental/ˌnjʊərəʊdɪˌvɛləpˈmɛnt(ə)l/ *adj.* 關於神經發展的

• The **neurodevelopmental** research has been putting to a halt due to a lack of government funding.

由於缺乏政府的資助，關於神經發展的研究已經中止了。

PART 1 雅思精選必考字彙

PART 2 實力檢測 Vocabulary in Context

Unit 2《劍 14》
Test 1 Reading Passage 2

The Growth of Bike-sharing Schemes around the world
世界各地共享腳踏車計畫的成長

• KEY 13 ⦿ ▶ MP3 02

-- scheme /sk'im/ *n.* 方案、計劃、組合、系統、圖解、摘要、詭計、陰謀；*vt. vi.* 計劃、設計、圖謀、策劃

- A honey plot is a **scheme** frequently used in various circumstances, but sometimes it is futile.

  美人計是在不同的情況下頻繁被使用的計謀，但是有時候卻是無效的。

• KEY 14

-- oppose /əp'oz/ *vt.* 反對、以...對抗、抗爭；*vi.* 反對

- Due to the sanitation issues and other concerns, the new beverage will be strongly **opposed** by government officials.

  由於衛生議題和其他的考量，新的飲料將受到政府官員們的強烈反對。

KEY 15

-- symbolic /sɪmbˈɑlɪk/ *adj.* 象徵性的、象徵手法的、象徵派的

● His **symbolic** way of delineating the nude lady has earned many accolades from a group of professors.

他象徵式的描繪裸體女性手法已經從一群教授們那裡贏得許多稱讚。

KEY 16

-- elaborate /ɪlˈæbrət/ *adj.* 精細的、詳盡的、精心的

● Ancestors of the village had an **elaborate** notion about herbs and medicine.

村子裡的祖先們過去對於草藥和醫學有著詳盡的想法。

KEY 17

-- municipality / mj,unɪsəpˈæləti/ *n.* 自治區、市當局、全市民

● The **municipality** has abrogated lengthy procedures, making local residents more convenient.

市當局已經廢除冗長的程序，讓當地的居民更為便利。

KEY 18

-- distribute /dɪstrˈɪbjut/ *vt.* 分配、分發、分佈、散佈、分類

● Meat will be evenly **distributed** to every household after the festival.

肉品將會在節慶後均分給每個家庭。

KEY 19

-- unanimously /jun'ænəməsli/ *adv.* 無異議地；同意地

- Interviewers of the preliminary screening all **unanimously** voted against hiring candidate A, but the CEO insisted on interviewing him.

初選的面試官們一致對於 A 候選人投下了反對雇用票，但是 CEO 卻堅持要面試他。

KEY 20

-- glorious /gl'ɔriəs/ *adj.* 光榮的；輝煌的、燦爛的；令人愉快的

- The **glorious** chapter of his career includes his five promotions in six years.

他榮耀的職涯篇章包含了他在六年內的五次升遷。

KEY 21

-- conspicuous /kənsp'ɪkjuəs/ *adj.* 顯著的、顯眼的、出眾的

- Angry chameleons are quite **conspicuous** in the forests since their coloration has changed from forest green to blazing red.

生氣的變色龍在森林中顯得相當引人注目，因為牠們的顏色已經從森林綠轉成炙烈的紅色。

KEY 22

-- vandalism /v'ændəlɪzəm/ *n.* 對藝術的破壞

- The skillful and unprecedented design on the wall of the

City Council is ruled by the judge as **vandalism**.

在市議會牆上史無前例且精心製作的設計被法官評定為是對藝術的破壞。

KEY 23

-- abolish /əbˈɑlɪʃ/ *vt.* 廢止、革除、取消

- **Abolishing** the age limit for attending the language aptitude test is still debatable.

廢除參加語言性向測驗的年紀限制仍然是受爭論的。

KEY 24

-- mentality /mɛntˈæləti/ *n.* 精神力、智力、頭腦作用、思想

- He is such an intelligent baby, an infant with above average **mentality**, scoring consistently high in the IQ test.

他是如此聰明的嬰孩，有著高於一般平均的智力，在 IQ 測驗上持續性地獲取高分。

Unit 3 《劍 14》
Test 1 Reading Passage 3

Motivational Factors and the Hospitality Industry
激勵因素和觀光服務業

KEY 25 ▶ MP3 03

-- originate /ə'ɪdʒən,et/ *v.* 發自；*vt.* 開始、發明、發起；*vi.* 發源、發生

- This bamboo dish was **originated** from China and was later modified to the new gourmet that we see today.
  這道竹筍菜餚原創於中國而於稍後修改成我們今日所見到的新美食。

KEY 26

-- emphasize /'ɛmfəs,aɪz/ *vt.* 強調、加強語氣、著重

- **Emphasizing** your strength during an interview can be a good thing.
  在面試期間，強調你的強項可能是件好事。

KEY 27

-- specifically /spəs'ɪfɪkli/ *adv.* 特別地、具體地

- Writing your resume in a **specifically** way can do you more good than harm.

以具體地方式撰寫履歷表對於你本身來説可能是利多於弊的。

• KEY 28

-- extend /ɪkst'ɛnd/ *vt.* 延長、延伸；擴大、擴充；給予、表示；
vi. 伸展、擴大、延續

- The government has decided to **extend** the health care to someone who is single.

政府已經決定將健康照護延伸至單身族群。

• KEY 29

-- underdeveloped /ˌʌndə·dɪv'ɛləpt/ *adj.* 開發不充分的

- The doctor still has not told the couple the truth that the brain of their newborn baby might be **underdeveloped**.

醫生仍未告知那對夫妻他們的新生小孩可能發展不完全。

• KEY 30

-- substance /s'ʌbstəns/ *n.* 物質

- The chemical **substance** in this type of wild flowers is extremely poisonous.

存在於這類型野花裡的化學物質是具有異常劇毒的。

• KEY 31

-- constructive /kənstr'ʌktɪv/ *adj.* 建設性的、構造上的、作圖的

- A **constructive** criticism is better than vindictive and hurtful comments.

  一則具建設性的批評比報復性和傷人的評論好得多了。

• KEY 32

-- recurring /rɪkˈɚɪŋ/ *adj.* 循環發生的

- Mistakes in the office can be **recurring** if the procedures are not meticulously monitored.

  如果程序沒有小心翼翼地監控的話，辦公室中的錯誤可能會是循環發生的。

• KEY 33

-- succinctly /səksˈɪŋktli/ *adv.* 簡潔地

- Writing your resume in a **succinctly** way can save HR personnel quite some time.

  以簡潔地方式撰寫你的履歷表能夠節省人事專員相當多的時間。

• KEY 34

-- retention /ritˈɛnʃən/ *n.* 保留、保持

- Talent **retention** has been hard in the economic boom, but quite easy in the economic downturn.

  在經濟繁榮時，人才留用挺困難，但於景氣蕭條時卻相當容易。

• KEY 35

-- predisposition /prˌidɪspəzˈɪʃən/ *n.* 傾向、氣質

- The **predisposition** of the young lady is the main reason that she gets favored by the director.

  這位年輕女士的氣質是她受到總裁偏好的原因。

• KEY 36

-- inherently /ɪnh'ɪrəntli/ *adv.* 天性地；固有地

- Proponents of this theory are arguing that people are not **inherently** bad.

  這個理論的支持者正爭論著人們的天性並非與生俱來就是壞的。

Unit 4 《劍 14》
Test 2 Reading Passage 1

Alexander Henderson
亞歷山大・韓德遜

• KEY 37 ▶ MP3 04

-- merchant /mˈɚtʃənt/ *n.* 商人

- The **merchant** has enormous wealth due to his diplomatic relationships with several leaders in the area.

    由於他與幾位此地區的領導者有著外交關係，這位商人有巨大的財富。

• KEY 38

-- extensive /ɪkstˈɛnsɪv/ *adj.* 廣的、廣泛的、多方面的

- His **extensive** interests and hobbies make him harder to narrow down his focus and later pursuit.

    他廣泛的興趣和嗜好讓他較難於稍後的追求中窄化他的專注項目。

• KEY 39

-- landholding /lˈændh,oldɪŋ/ *n.* 土地所有

- The Judge has ruled in favor for the government, deeming that the **landholding** is not belonged to the local residents.
  法官已經判定政府這方勝訴，認為土地所有權不屬於當地居民們。

🔑 KEY 40

-- residence /ˈrɛzɪdəns/ *n.* 居住、留駐、存在、住宅、宅第
- The **residence** near the tropical rainforest is a tourist spot, and is quite an important layover for multiple visitors.
  在熱帶雨林附近的住宅是觀光勝地，對於許多拜訪者來說是相當重要的短暫停留處。

🔑 KEY 41

-- outskirt /ˈaʊtskˌɚt/ *n.* 邊界、郊外、外區
- In the **outskirt** of the small town, there are only a few neighborhoods, so you have to prepare enough food and drinks.
  在小鎮的郊區，僅有幾戶人家住著，所以你必須要準備足夠的食物和飲用水。

🔑 KEY 42

-- apprenticeship /əprˈɛntəsˌ ɪp/ *n.* 學徒的身分、學徒的年限
- The **apprenticeship** has now extended to more than five years, more lenient than before.
  學徒的年限已經延長到超過五年了，比起之前來說更為寬裕。

•KEY 43

-- emigrate /'ɛməgr,et/ *vi. vt.* （使）移居、（使）移民

- The family of Chen **emigrated** to Australia years ago, leaving the farm uncultivated and desolate.

  陳姓一家人幾年前移居到澳洲了，遺留著未耕作和荒廢的農田。

•KEY 44

-- excursion /ɪksk'ɚʒən/ *n.* 遠足、遊覽、短程旅行

- All pupils are so excited to learn that they will be having five **excursions** in a year.

  所有小學生在得知他們在一年內將會有五次遠足感到非常興奮。

•KEY 45

-- chairman /tʃ'ɛrmən/ *n.* 主席、會長

- The **chairman** of the company has the brain tumor removed, but his health condition is still not good.

  公司的董事長已經將腦瘤移除了，但是他的健康狀況仍然不是很好。

•KEY 46

-- circulation /s'ɚkjəl,eʃən/ *n.* 流通、循環、發行量

- The **circulation** of the newspaper has dwindled to only 5,000 copies in the first print.

  報紙的發行量在首刷時已經降至僅有五千份了。

• KEY 47

-- document /dˈɑkjəmɛnt/ *n.* 文檔、公文、文件、文獻；証件、証券；紀錄影片、記實小説；*vt.* 用文件証明

- The **document** went abruptly missing, scaring multiple executives because it was the only copy.
文件突然不見嚇到眾多主管，因為那是唯一的副本。

• KEY 48

-- construction/kənstrˈʌkʃən/ *n.* 建造、建築、建設【U】；建築物、建造物【C】

- The **construction** site has remained unused due to a sudden court order by the prosecutor five months ago.
由於五個月前檢察官突然出示的法庭令，建築地點仍維未使用。

Unit 5 《劍 14》
Test 2 Reading Passage 2

Back to the Future of Skyscraper design
回到摩天大廈設計的未來

KEY 49  ▶ MP3 05

-- culmination /kˌʌlmən'eʃən/ *n.* 頂點、極點、最高點

• Surprisingly, the film has reached its **culmination** in an opening scene, astounding most audiences.

令人感到意外的是，電影在開場就達到了高峰，讓大多數的觀眾感到驚訝。

KEY 50

-- gadget /g'ædʒət/ *n.* 小配件、小玩意、詭計

• The **gadget** is actually a plus for the selling, since most consumers find it eye-catching.

小配件對於銷售實際上是加分的，因為大多數的消費者的目光都會被吸引。

KEY 51

-- squander /skw'ɑndɚ/ *vt.* 浪費、使分散；*vi.* 浪費、漂泊、四散

- College graduates often **squander** the first few years of their salaries, not knowing that money is hard-earned.

  大學畢業生通常會浪費掉他們前幾年的薪水，沒有意識到錢是難賺的。

• KEY 52

-- reinvention /ɪnvˈɛnʃən/ *n.* 再發明、再創造

- Most career advisors will suggest job-applicants that **reinvention** be the key to their future paths.

  大多數的職涯諮詢師會建議求職者再創造，這是他們未來道路的關鍵點。

• KEY 53

-- reliance /rɪlˈaɪəns/ *n.* 依賴、依靠、信心、信賴、信任

- **Reliance** on the import goods makes peddlers pretty unstable.

  仰賴進口商品讓小販們相當不穩定。

• KEY 54

-- accommodate /əkˈɑmədˌet/ *vt.* 使適應、調節、和解、容納；
vi. 適應

- For a new recruit, **accommodating** into an unfamiliar environment is not that easy.

  對於一個新的聘僱人員，適應一個不熟悉的環境並不是那麼容易的。

KEY 55

-- habitable /h'æbətəbəl/ *adj.* 可居住的

- Some parts of the forest have been cleared out, making this place not **habitable** for multiple birds and insects.

  森林的有些部分已經清除了，這使得這個地方不適宜眾多的鳥類和昆蟲居住了。

KEY 56

-- completely /kəmpl'itli/ *adv.* 完全地、十分地、全然

- Swimming in a dark murky lake has given Tom a **completely** novel experience.

  在黑暗隱蔽的湖泊裡游泳給予湯姆全然的新體驗。

KEY 57

-- disappearance /d,ɪsəp'ɪrəns/ *n.* 看不見、失蹤、消失

- The sudden **disappearance** of over five billion bees makes thousands of acres of fruits unfertilized.

  超過 50 億隻蜜蜂的突然消失讓數千畝的水果無法授粉。

KEY 58

-- clamor /kl'æmɚ/ *n.* 喧鬧、叫嚷、大聲的要求；*vi. vt.* 喧嚷、大聲的要求

- The **clamor** of the night market is the main reason why he wants to relocate.

  夜市的喧鬧是他想要重新移居的主要原因。

• KEY 59

-- naturally /nˈætʃɚəli/ *adv.* 自然地、以自然力、天生地

- Cindy is **naturally** beautiful, so she does not need any makeup.

  辛蒂天生麗質，所以她不需要任何化妝品。

• KEY 60

-- comparable /kˈɑmpɚəbəl/ *adj.* 可以相比的、比得上的、可匹敵的

- The only horse that can be **comparable** to Guan Yu is Red Hare.

  能夠與關羽匹配的唯一馬匹是赤兔馬。

Unit 6 《劍 14》
Test 2 Reading Passage 3

Why Companies Should Welcome Disorder
為什麼公司要樂於接受混亂呢？

▶ KEY 61  ▶MP3 06

-- productive /prəd'ʌktɪv/ *adj.* 能生產的、有生產價值的、多產的

- A **productive** land can generate more dollars than an unproductive one.

  一個多產土地比起不具生產力的土地能產出更多的價值。

▶ KEY 62

-- countless /k'aʊntləs/ *adj.* 數不盡的、無數的

- **Countless** swordsmen are hidden behind the huge rocks waiting for a surprise attack.

  數之不盡的武士藏匿在巨石後方，等待突襲。

▶ KEY 63

-- massively /m'æsɪvli/ *adv.* 巨大地、重地的、堅實地

- As a result of the approaching typhoon, rainfall dropped **massively**, pouring all over the streets.

由於颱風的迫近，雨勢滂沱，傾注在所有的街道上。

• KEY 64

-- steadily /stˈɛdəli/ *adv.* 穩定地、無變化地、有規則地

- The yield of the watermelons has increased steadily over the year, making farmers relatively thrilled.

西瓜的產量在這些年已經有著穩定的增加，這讓農夫們相當地興奮。

• KEY 65

-- forefather /fˈɔrfˌɑðɚ/ *n.* 祖先

- The **forefather** was wise enough to use certain blends in this dish to neutralize sour flavor.

祖先有智慧到在這道菜餚中使用特定的混和，以中和掉酸味。

• KEY 66

-- misguided /mɪsgˈɑɪdɪd/ *adj.* 被誤導的

- Instructions given by amateur swimmers can be unprofessional, making students feel **misguided**.

業餘游泳員們給予的指示可能是不專業的，這讓學生們覺得被誤導了。

• KEY 67

-- diminishing /dɪmˈɪnɪʃɪŋ/ *adj.* 遞減的

- The population of crabs has been **diminishing** due to

sweltering hot summer and the increasing number of octopuses.

由於悶熱的夏天和逐漸增加的章魚數量，使得螃蟹族群數量持續減少。

• KEY 68

-- outweigh /ˈaʊtwˌe/ *v.* 比...為重、比...重要、比...有價值

- Getting the highest remark in the written still cannot **outweigh** the overall impression during the interview.

在筆試中獲取最高的分數仍無法勝過在面試期間的整體印象。

• KEY 69

-- bottleneck /bˈatəlnˌɛk/ *n.* 瓶頸

- A pride of lions has encountered a **bottleneck** when they are about to cross the river.

獅群在跨越河岸時面臨到瓶頸。

• KEY 70

-- disorganization /dɪsˌɔrgənəzˈeʃən/ *n.* 組織的破壞、解體、瓦解

- A herd of buffalos seems unified and robust, but the situation is going to have a **disorganization** by lions' ambush and surprise attack.

一群水牛似乎統一且強壯，但是在遭遇獅子的埋伏和突襲後正面臨瓦解。

• KEY 71

-- hierarchy /h'aɪɚ,ɑrki/ *n.* 階層

- The **hierarchy** of the pyramid exhibits relationships among producers, consumers, and apex predators.

  金字塔的階層，展示出生產者、消費者和頂端掠食者的關係。

• KEY 72

-- venerate /v'ɛnɚ,et/ *v.* 尊敬、崇敬、崇拜

- Villagers **venerate** their gods so much that anyone who is disrespectful to them will get punished severely.

  村落的人很尊敬他們的神明以至於任何對其不敬人將受到嚴懲。

Unit 7 《劍 14》
Test 3 Reading Passage 1

The Concept of Intelligence
智力的概念

• KEY 73  ▶ MP3 07

-- implicit /ɪmpl'ɪsət/ *adj.* 暗示的、盲從的、含蓄的、固有的、絕對的

- The CEO talks in a very **implicit** way, not wanting to hurt anyone's feelings.
  這位 CEO 以很含蓄的方式表達，不想要傷害任何人的感受。

• KEY 74

-- intelligence /ɪnt'ɛlədʒəns/ *n.* 智力、聰明、理解力；情報、諜報；資訊

- Octopuses have been known for their high **intelligence**, ink, and remarkable camouflage.
  章魚以牠們高度的智力、墨水和驚人的偽裝聞名。

• KEY 75

-- conceptualize /kən`sɛptʃʊəl,aɪz/ *v.* 使有概念

- To assist learners to **conceptualize** the notion of physics, the professor designed a huge planetary model with several mathematical formulas labelling on the side.

  為了協助學習者對於物理觀念有概念，教授設計了一個巨型的行星模型，裡頭有著幾個數學公式。

KEY 76

-- phenomenon /fən'amən,an/ *n.* 現象、特殊的人、特殊的事物、奇跡

- The phenomenon that hornets attacking bee colonies is very common.

  大黃蜂群攻擊蜜蜂群的現象是非常普遍的。

KEY 77

-- correspondence /k,ɔrəsp'andəns/ *n.* 對應、一致、符合；通信、信函、信件

- The **correspondence** has now become the proof of the treason crime, and he is now facing a life-long exclusion of the United States.

  信件現在已經成了叛國罪的證據，而他正面臨終生無法入境美國的刑期。

KEY 78

-- elucidate /ɪl'usəd,et/ *vt.* 闡明、說明

- There are still several things for the criminal to **elucidate** so that the prosecutor will know whether he is guilty or not.

仍然有幾件事情需要釐清，這樣一來檢控官就會知道他是否有罪了。

• KEY 79

-- irresponsible /ɪrəsp'ansəbəl/ *adj.* 不負責任的、不可靠的

- **Irresponsible** parents, like cuckoos, leave their babies for other birds to nurture.

不負責任的父母，就像是杜鵑鳥，將牠們的小孩留給其他鳥類養育。

• KEY 80

-- unintelligent /ˌʌnɪnˈtɛlədʒənt / *adj.* 缺乏才智的；無知的；愚蠢的

- The **unintelligent** snake walks into striking distance of the spider.

愚蠢的蛇，步入蜘蛛的攻擊範圍內。

• KEY 81

-- competency /ˈkampətənsɪ / *n.* 能力

- The newly recruits are given different tasks in accordance with their **competencies**.

新聘人員將會根據他們的能力賦予不同類型的任務。

• KEY 82

-- presupposition /pr,ɪsəpəz'ɪʃən/ *n.* 預想、假定、前提

• The **presupposition** is a great hindrance for scientists who having been developing the drug for years.

預想對於已經研發這項藥物有好幾年的科學家來說是個很大的阻礙。

• KEY 83

-- experimental /ɪksp,ɛrəm'ɛntəl/ *adj.* 實驗的、根據實驗的

• The chemical reagent is still **experimental**, so an injection can still be considered risky and destructive.

化學試劑仍在試驗中,所以注射仍可能被視為是具有風險且具破壞性的。

• KEY 84

-- scientific /s,ɑɪənt'ɪfɪk/ *adj.* 科學的;符合科學規律的、精確的

• Without **scientific** evidence, it is hard to convince the jury that the drug can be therapeutic.

缺乏科學證據,很難令陪審團信服這個藥物具有療效。

Unit 8 《劍 14》
Test 3 Reading Passage 2

Save Bugs to Find New Drugs
拯救昆蟲以發掘新藥物

• KEY 85  ▶ MP3 08

-- deter /dɪt'ə/ *vt.* 制止、使斷念、威懾

• To **deter** his son to get married with a much older woman, she sent his son away to pursue a higher learning in Europe.

為了阻止他的兒子與較年長的女性結婚，她將他兒子送往歐洲更高學府求學。

• KEY 86

-- noxious /n'ɑkʃəs/ *adj.* 有害的、有毒的、精神不健全的

• **Noxious** flowers can cause impairment to our breathing ability and an increase in blood pressure.

有毒的花朵會對於我們的呼吸能力造成損害以及血壓的升高。

• KEY 87

-- pharmaceutical /f,ɑrməs'utɪkəl/ *adj.* 配藥學的

- The **pharmaceutical** company has deliberately used strategies to blindside the prosecutor so that they will win over the heart of the jury.

  藥品公司已經故意地使用策略，出其不意地打擊檢控官，這樣一來他們就能能贏得陪審團的心。

• KEY 88

-- modification /mˌɑdəfək'eʃən/ *n.* 修正、修飾、修改

- The **modification** of the menu has made the restaurant more popular than ever.

  菜單的修改已讓餐廳比往常更為熱門。

• KEY 89

-- hurdle /h'ɚdəl/ *v.* 障礙、跳欄、臨時活動籬笆；*vt.* 用籬笆圍、越過、克服

- The **hurdle** in the first few years are tremendous, but after those years, it will become relatively effortless.

  在頭幾年障礙很巨大，但之後就會變得相當不費吹灰之力。

• KEY 90

-- looming /l'umɪŋ/ *adj.* 幽影

- The **looming** in the desert makes it easy to believe that there is actually an oasis there.

  沙漠中的幽影很容易讓人相信那裡實際上有綠洲的存在。

PART 1 雅思精選必考字彙

PART 2 實力檢測 Vocabulary in Context

• KEY 91

-- undisputed /ˌʌndɪˈspjutɪd/ *adj.* 無可爭辯的；毫無疑問的

• That professional athletes have a better shot than amateurs is **undisputed**.

專業的運動員比起業餘運動員有較佳的勝率這點是無可爭辯的。

• KEY 92

-- enormous /ɪnˈɔrməs/ *adj.* 巨大的、龐大的

• The company has **enormous** of loans and bills to pay, making banks doubting its ability to repay the money.

公司有巨大的貸款和帳單要付，這讓銀行懷疑該公司的還款能力。

• KEY 93

-- tiny /tˈɑɪni/ *adj.* 極小的、微小的

• A **tiny** portion of the local residents eat beef, so the restaurants seldom have beef-related dishes on the menu.

當地居民的極小部分吃牛肉，所以餐廳幾乎沒有牛肉相關的菜餚。

• KEY 94

-- secrete /sɪkrˈit/ *v.* 隱秘、隱藏、隱匿、分泌

• Certain plants **secrete** sweet and juicy juice to lure the pollinators.

特定的植物分泌甜且多汁的汁液引誘授粉者。

• KEY 95

-- ubiquity /jub'ɪkwɪti/ *n.* 到處存在、遍在、耶穌的遍在

• Due to increasing squirrels in the area, they have increased the **ubiquity** of the seeds of fruits.

由於該地區日益增多的松鼠，松鼠們已經提高了水果種子遍布的情況。

• KEY 96

-- infrequently /ɪnfr'ikwəntli/ *adv.* 稀少地、珍貴地

• Flying sea birds **infrequently** visit the cliffs, making flowers of the cliffs exceedingly rare and expensive.

飛翔的海鳥罕見地拜訪懸崖峭壁，讓峭壁上的花朵變得異常稀有且昂貴。

PART 1 雅思精選必考字彙

PART 2 實力檢測 Vocabulary in Context

Unit 9 《劍 14》
Test 3 Reading Passage 3

The Power of Play
玩耍的力量

🔑 KEY 97    ▶ MP3 09

-- counterpart /kʼaʊntɚpˌɑrt/ *n.* 副本、復本、配對物、相應物

- Northern **counterparts** do not have as many medicinal components as the local ones.
  北方的聚落沒有當地聚落具有那麼多樣的醫療要件。

🔑 KEY 98

-- preparation /prˌɛpɚʼeʃən/ *n.* 准備、預備、配製、配置品、准備工作

- The **preparation** of the dish can take more than six hours, so normally it is served during major festivals.
  這項菜餚的準備時間要超過六小時,所以通常在節慶期間才會出這道菜。

🔑 KEY 99

-- dichotomy /daɪkʼatəmi/ *n.* 兩分、分裂、二分法

- The **dichotomy** of separating the lists of candidates might be unfair, but it will curtail the screening process.

  區分列表上的候選人的二分法可能不公平，但是此舉將縮減篩選流程的時間。

• KEY 100

-- consensus /kəns'ɛnsəs/ *n.* 一致、共識

- It is hard to reach a **consensus** if both parties cannot have the same goal in mind.

  如果雙方都沒有相同的目標的話，很難達成共識。

• KEY 101

-- elude /ɪl'ud/ *vt.* 逃避、規避、使困惑

- To **elude** the prosecution, he dresses himself like a nun and hides himself in a remote temple.

  為了逃避起訴，他將自己裝扮成尼姑而且藏匿在遙遠的廟宇裡。

• KEY 102

-- discrete /dɪskr'it/ *adj.* 離散的、不連續的

- You can find a **discrete** but not continuous stripes on this tiger's back.

  你可以在老虎的背上發現離散不連續的斑紋。

• KEY 103

-- purposeless /p'ɚpəsləs/ *adj.* 無目的的、無意義的

- Being **purposeless** in a job can be quite harmful for one's career.

  在工作中漫無目的對於一個人的職涯是有相當程度的傷害。

• KEY 104

-- intrinsic /ıntr'ınsık/ *adj.* 本質的、原有的、真正的
- The farm restaurant has lost its **intrinsic** values because of the sudden pouring of cash and growing visitors.

  因為突然湧現的現金和日益增多的拜訪者，農場餐廳已經失去了原有的價值。

• KEY 105

-- continuum /kənt'ınjuəm/ *n.* 連續、連續統、閉聯集
- Three kingdoms are a long continuum, not something that happens in a day.

  三國是經由長期演變而成的，並非一日之間發生的。

• KEY 106

-- playfulness /pl'efəlnəs/ *n.* 玩笑、嬉鬧
- **Playfulness** is quite essential for wild animals if they want to survive to adulthood.

  嬉鬧對於野生動物來說是相當重要的，如果他們想要存活至成年時期的話。

• KEY 107

-- extrinsically /ɛk`strɪnsɪk!ɪ/ *adv.* 非本質地；外部上；外來地

• If children need to be motivated **extrinsically**, their progress and academic success can come to a halt when there are no monetary incentives.

如果小孩需要外部因素驅策的話，他們的進步和學術成就可能在沒有金錢的誘因時就開始停滯了。

• KEY 108

-- healthy /h'ɛlθi/ *adj.* 健康的、健壯的、健全的、有益於健康的

• The **healthy** food was later found quite detrimental to our health.

這款健康的食物經稍後的查證後發現對於我們的健康是相當有害的。

Unit 10 《劍 14》
Test 4 Reading Passage 1

The Secret of Staying Young
維持年輕的秘訣

• KEY 109 ▶ MP3 10

-- immortal /ɪmˈɔrtəl/ *n.* 不朽的人物；*adj.* 永遠的、不死的、神的

• Matsu is considered by many an **immortal** goddess protecting thousands of sea sailors.

馬祖被許多人視為是不朽的女神，保護數以千計的航海員。

• KEY 110

-- reproduce /rˌɪprədˈus/ *vt.* 復制、翻版；再生產、再造;繁殖、生殖；*vi.* 繁殖、生殖;再生產、復制

• To **reproduce** the same recipe is impossible since all the original manuscripts were lost hundreds of years ago.

要複製出同樣的食譜是不可能的，因為所有的原稿都於數百年前遺失了。

• KEY 111

-- decline /dɪklˈɑɪn/ *v.* 衰微、跌落、下降；*vt.* 使降低、婉謝；*vi.*

下降、衰落、偏斜

- There was a significant **decline** in the number of octopuses in open sea due to excessive hunting activities.

在開放的海洋中，過度的捕獵活動，使得章魚數量有顯著的減少。

KEY 112

-- deteriorate /dɪt'ɪriə,et/ *vt. vi.* （使）惡化

- Without natural predators, the ecological balance has **deteriorated** to a certain degree, making the prairie denuded.

缺乏天敵，生態的平衡已經惡化到特定的程度了，這使得大草原呈現裸露的狀態。

KEY 113

-- complexity /kəmpl'ɛksəti/ *n.* 復雜、復雜性、復雜的事物

- **Complexity** of the food web is relevant to the stability of the ecosystem.

食物網的複雜度與生態系統的穩定度有關。

KEY 114

-- healthier /h'ɛlθiɚ/ *adj.* 較健康的

- To be **healthier**, the male model quits consuming diet pills and starts eating vegetables and fruits.

為了更健康，男性模特兒戒掉了服用減肥藥並開始食用蔬菜和水

果。

• KEY 115

-- respond /rɪsp'ɑnd/ *vt.* 回答；*vi.* 回答、響應、回報、有反應、承擔責任

- The police are **responding** to the event pretty seriously, since a huge blaze had engulfed a hundred people.
  警方對於此事件的回應相當嚴肅，因為巨大的烈焰吞噬了一百個人。

• KEY 116

-- experiment /ɪksp'ɛrəmənt/ *n.* 實驗、試驗；*vi.* 進行實驗、做試驗

- The **experiment** is too laborious, so many scientists have abdicated to do the continued research in this month.
  實驗太費力了，所以在這個月許多科學家已經放棄要繼續做研究。

• KEY 117

-- coincide /k,ɔɪns'aɪd/ *v.* 巧合、重合、一致、符合

- The number of lost diamonds was found under the sea floor, and the number **coincides** with the 1989 museum records of 109.
  遺失的鑽石數量於海洋底部找到了，而數量跟 1989 年博物館所記錄的數量 109 顆正好吻合。

•KEY 118

-- decrease /dɪkr'is/ *vi.* 減少、減小；*vt.* 減少、減小

- The number of people visiting museums **decreased** in 2018, but has a remarkable boost in the following year.

  參觀博物館的人數於 2018 年減少，但是次年有著顯著的增加。

•KEY 119

-- comfort /k'ʌmfɚt/ *n.* 舒適、安逸【U】；慰問、安慰【C】；*vt.* 慰問、安慰

- Villagers find the latest-built hotel quite exquisite, and the **comfort** of the room somehow eases their weary bodies.

  村民發現最新建造的旅館相當精緻，而房間的舒適度不知怎麼的減緩了他們疲憊的身軀。

•KEY 120

-- extend /ɪkst'ɛnd/ *vt.* 延長、延伸；擴大、擴充；給予、表示；*vi.* 伸展、擴大、延續

- The government has decided to **extend** the compulsory education to university so that the literacy transcends some international countries.

  政府已經決定要將義務教育延長至大學，這樣一來識字率就會超過有些國際性的國家。

Unit 11 《劍 14》
Test 4 Reading Passage 2

Why Zoos Are Good
為什麼動物園是有益的呢?

KEY 121 ▶ MP3 11

-- quality /kwˈɑləti/ *n.* 品質、特質、才能、質量

- To win the heart of consumers, **quality** of the product is very vital.

  為了贏得消費者的心,產品的品質是非常重要的。

KEY 122

-- supplement /sˈʌpləmənt/ *n.* 補充物、增刊、補充,*vt.* 補充、增補

- **Supplements**, such as vitamins tablets and juice, are quite essential for someone who is lack of minerals in his daily consumption.

  補給品,例如維他命錠和果汁對於一些在日常攝取中缺乏礦物質的人來說相當重要。

• KEY 123

-- movement /m'uvmənt/ *n.* 運動、動作、運轉、移動、傾向、變化、活動、樂章

• The **movement** of the rotated machines in the farmland produces unnecessary noise.

在農地，轉動機械產生不必要的噪音。

• KEY 124

-- starvation /stɑrv'eʃən/ *n.* 飢餓、餓死

• In war-torn countries, **starvation** is so unavoidable, and there is no food left, except decayed carcasses.

在飽受戰爭摧殘的國家中，飢餓是無可避免的。沒有食物留存，只剩一些已經受蝕的屍體。

• KEY 125

-- automatically /ˌɔtəm'ætɪkli/ *adv.* 自動地、機械地

• The uncultivated farmland has become fertile and restored thanks to the machine that **automatically** runs on it.

未耕種的農地已經變得肥沃且狀態復原，多虧了農地上的機器在上頭自動地翻動著。

• KEY 126

-- threaten /θr'ɛtən/ *vt.* 威脅、恐嚇、恫嚇；預示…的凶兆；*vi.* 威脅、恐嚇、恫嚇

• Surprisingly, honey badgers are gallant and combative

enough to **threaten** lions.

令人感到意外的是，蜜獾勇敢和具戰鬥性到足以威嚇獅子。

• KEY 127

-- unexpected /ˌʌnɪksp'ɛktɪd/ *adj.* 料想不到的、突然的、意外的

- The result of the interview is quite **unexpected** because no one gets hired.

面試的結果相當地意外，因為沒有人被雇用。

• KEY 128

-- reservoir /r'ɛzəvwˋɑr/ *n.* 貯水池、貯藏處、貯備、水庫；*vt.* 儲藏

- The huge understory basement can be quite a **reservoir** for buckets of high-quality red wine.

巨大的底層地下室可能是相當有份量的儲存槽，存放著高品質的紅酒。

• KEY 129

-- specimen/sp'ɛsəmən/ *n.* 樣品、標本、試料

- Linda was accused of stealing the jewelry **specimen** from another company.

琳達被控於從另一間公司偷竊珠寶標本。

• KEY 130

-- conservation /kˌɑnsəv'eʃən/ *n.* 保存、保護；守恆、不滅

- **Conservation** efforts for whales are needed because lots of illegal hunting are rampant these days.

  努力保護鯨魚是必須的，因為這些日子以來非法盜獵非常猖獗。

• KEY 131

-- bolster /b'olstɚ/ *v.* 支援、長枕；*vt.* 支援、支撐

- To bolster his confidence, the friend listed numerous companies that actually valued his specialty.

  為了增強他的自信，朋友列出了很多公司實際上珍視他的專長。

• KEY 132

-- reduction /rəd'ʌkʃən/ *n.* 縮小、減少、降低；簡化、簡約；還原、復原

- A significant **reduction** in the number of people consuming in the coffee shops has led to closure of shops in the area.

  在咖啡店消費的人數的顯著下滑已經導致這個地區的數間店結束營業。

Unit 12 《劍 14》
Test 4 Reading Passage 3

Ecological Research
生態研究

· KEY 133 ▶ MP3 12

-- dismal /dˈɪzməl/ *adj.* 陰沈的、淒涼的、暗的、低落的情緒、沼澤

- Removing the livestock from a **dismal** farmland is actually a good thing.
  實際上，將牲畜從陰暗的農地中移除是件好事。

· KEY 134

-- collection /kəlˈɛkʃən/ *n.* 收集、聚集、積累、收藏

- The **collection** of wine can be laborious, but the showcase of the cellar and the wine turns out to be worthwhile and enjoyable.
  酒的收藏可能是費力的，但是展示地窖和酒終究證實是值得且令人感到愉快的。

• KEY 135

-- determine /dət'əmən/ *vt.* 決定、決心；確定、限定、測定；使決定；*vi.* 決定、決心

• To **determine** who is the real killer, the jury has reached a verdict by adopting the latest evidence brought by prosecutors this morning.

為了決定誰是真的殺手，陪審團已經藉由採用由檢控官們今天早晨所提出的最新證據達成了判決。

• KEY 136

-- examine /ɪgz'æmɪn/ *vt.* 檢查、細查;對…進行考試；*vi.* 檢查、細查、調查

• The Judge has requested the defense to **examine** toxicity of different fruits and submit the report tomorrow afternoon.

法官已經要求辯方去檢視不同水果中的毒性並且於明日下午遞交報告。

• KEY 137

-- validity /vəl'ɪdəti/ *n.* 有效性、正確性

• The **validity** of the test is being questioned by numerous scholars.

考試的有效性被許多學者們質疑。

• KEY 138

-- investigation /ɪnvˈɛstəgˈeʃən/ *n.* 調查、審查、研究

- While the **investigation** is still going on, the attorney has refused to talk about anything further about the case.

  既然調查仍在進行中，律師已經拒絕進一步談論任何關於這個案例。

• KEY 139

-- analysis /ənˈæləsəs/ *n.* 分解、分析、解析

- The **analysis** of the financial report remains unfinished since economists cannot seem to find an angle to start with.

  財務報告的分析仍未完成，因為經濟學者們無法找到一個可以切入的角度。

• KEY 140

-- pollution /pəlˈuʃən/ *n.* 污染、敗壞、弄髒

- The **pollution** is the main reason why a lot of birds will not have a layover during their migration.

  汙染是許多鳥類在牠們遷徙期間沒有短暫停留的主因。

• KEY 141

-- conjure /kˈandʒɚ/ *vt.* 以咒文召喚、變戲法、想象；*vi.* 變戲法、施魔法祈求、懇求

- The villagers have become so hopeless and pessimistic that they eventually turn to witches to **conjure** more rainfall for their town.

村民們已經變得如此的希望渺茫和悲觀以至於村民們最終轉向女巫們施魔法祈求小鎮的降雨。

• KEY 142

-- simulation /s'ɪmjəl'eʃən/ *n.* 模擬、偽裝、模仿

• After the tenth attempt, the **simulation** of the invaluable recipe is still a huge fiasco.

在第十次的嘗試後，價值連城的食譜的模仿仍舊是很大的災難。

• KEY 143

-- misperception /m'ɪspɚs'ɛpʃən/ *n.* 錯誤的理解或詮釋

• The **misperception** of the martial arts manuscripts can be deleterious to one's major organs.

武俠原稿的錯誤解讀可能對於一個人的主要器官有害。

• KEY 144

-- entanglement /ɛnt'æŋgəlmənt/ *n.* 糾纏、捲入、纏繞物

• The **entanglement** of the relationships among different characters has made audiences harder to grasp the ending.

幾個角色間的感情糾纏使得觀眾更難取掌握結局。

Unit 13 《劍 13》
Test 1 Reading Passage 1

Case Study: Tourism New Zealand Website
案例研究：紐西蘭旅遊網

• KEY 145 ▶ MP3 13

-- domestic /dəm'ɛstɪk/ *adj.* 家裏的、家庭的；本國的、國內的；馴養的

• **Domestic** livestock is still not enough for local needs, so importing some is perhaps the solution.
家畜對於當地的需求仍不夠，所以進口可能是個解決之道。

• KEY 146

-- export /'ɛkspɔrt/ *n. vt.* 輸出、出口、外銷；*vi.* 輸出物資

• High reliance on the **export** is not good for the long-term profit.
高度仰賴出口對於長期的獲利不是件好事。

• KEY 147

-- communicate /kəmj'unək,et/ *vt.* 傳送、傳達；*vi.* 通訊、通信、交流

- To **communicate** more effectively, villagers in the valley use several gestures and signal lanterns to convey messages.
  為了更有效地溝通，山谷中的村民們使用幾個姿勢和信號燈籠來傳達訊息。

• KEY 148

-- exhilarating /ɪgz'ɪlɚ,etɪŋ/ *adj.* 令人喜歡的、使人愉快的、爽快的

- The **exhilarating** news came when Cindy was in the shower, and she picked up her cellphone during the shower.
  辛蒂在淋浴時收到令人感到興奮的消息，而她在淋浴期間接起了她的手機。

• KEY 149

-- authentic /əθ'ɛntɪk/ *adj.* 真實的、可靠的、可信的

- Tourists are eager to visit this place because all ingredients for making the dish are **authentic**.
  觀光客們都很渴望拜訪這個地方因為所有製作這道菜餚的原料都很真實。

• KEY 150

-- database /d'etəb,es/ *n.* 資料庫

- The **database** for the types of wine in the area is still scarce, so the professor thinks that there are lots of intriguing things the research project can do.

在這個地區，各類型的酒的資料庫仍舊匱乏，所以教授認為有許多引人興趣的研究計畫可以做。

• KEY 151

-- audience /ˈɑdɪəns/ *n.* 聽眾、觀眾、讀者；謁見、接見；傾聽、聽取

- The **audience** cannot wait for the next episode because the storyline is unbelievably crafted.
  觀眾無法等待下一集因為故事情節是讓人難以置信地精心編織的。

• KEY 152

-- update /əpdˈet/ *vt.* 更新、使現代化、補充最新資料

- The farm owners have **updated** pieces of machinery, so the efficiency has become unbelievably fast.
  農場主人已經更新了數件機械，所以效率變得異常快速。

• KEY 153

-- accurate /ˈækjɚˌet/ *adj.* 准確的；精確的

- The merchant has a more **accurate** way to measure whether the jewelry is authentic or not.
  商人有更精確的方式來測量珠寶是否是貨真價實。

• KEY 154

-- blockbuster /blˈɑkbˈʌstɚ/ *n.* 一種破壞性特強的炸彈；大轟動

- The **blockbuster** film has created such a great sensation that every reporter is eager to write about the related topic.

  大轟動的電影已經造成了如此大的迴響以至於每個記者都很渴望寫相關的主題。

• KEY 155

-- highlight /h'aɪl'aɪt/ v. 突出加亮區、精彩場面；*vt.* 加亮、使顯著、以強光照射

- Farm owners want to **highlight** the healthy food, tranquility of the valley, and striking scenery.

  農場主人想要強調健康食物、山谷的寧靜和引人注目的風景。

• KEY 156

-- accommodation /ək'amͻd'eʃən/ *n.* 設備、膳宿、旅館房間；容納、提供、適應；調解、妥協

- **Accommodation** is still a problem for someone who cannot stand sleeping on the train.

  對於一些無法忍受在火車上睡覺的人來說，住宿仍舊是個問題。

Unit 14 《劍 13》
Test 1 Reading Passage 2

Why Being Bored Is Stimulating – and Useful, too
為什麼無聊是振奮人心且有用的呢？

KEY 157 ▶ MP3 14

-- boredom /bʼɔrdəm/ *n.* 厭煩、厭倦、令人厭煩的事物

• Doing repetitive tasks all day makes certain types of people feel bored; thus, flexible working hours are used to reduce the **boredom**.
整天都做重複性的任務讓特定類型的人感到無聊，因此，彈性的工時能用於減低無聊。

KEY 158

-- agitated /ʼædʒət,etəd/ *adj.* 躁動的

• When threatened or insecure, monkeys can be quite **agitated**.
當受到威脅或感到不安全感時，猴子會變得相當躁動。

KEY 159

-- calibrate /kʼæləbr,et/ *vt.* 測定口徑、校準、查看刻度、劃刻度

- During jungle hunting, the speed of calibrating the distance between the target and you is quite essential because impalas often move really fast.

  在叢林狩獵期間，校準目標距離的速度是相當重要的，因為黑斑羚通常移動得很快速。

• KEY 160

-- specialize /spˈɛʃəlˌaɪz/ *vt.* 使特殊化、列舉、特別指明、限定⋯的範圍；*vi.* 成為專家、專攻

- **Specializing** in a specific domain is one of the ways to get a higher salary.

  在特定領域內專攻是獲取較高薪資的唯一方式。

• KEY 161

-- arousal /əˈaʊzəl/ *n.* 覺醒、激勵

- Swimming sometimes gives people different levels of **arousal**, especially when different temperatures of water touch our body.

  游泳有時候給予人們不同程度的覺醒，特別是當不同溫度的水接觸到我們的身體時。

• KEY 162

-- creativity /krˌietˈɪvəti/ *n.* 創造力、創造

- These types of jobs require a high level of **creativity**.

  這些類型的工作需要高度的創意。

-- undesirable /ˌʌndɪzˈɑɪrəbəl/ *adj.* 不受歡迎的、不良的

- Wasps might be **undesirable** for desert chameleons since they have stings.

  黃蜂對於沙漠變色龍來說可能是不受歡迎的他們有刺。

• KEY 164

-- frustration /frəstrˈeʃən/ *n.* 打破、挫折、頓挫

- The **frustration** of not being able to hunt a chameleon leads to a kill towards another target.

  無法獵捕變色龍的挫折導致轉換去獵捕另一個目標。

• KEY 165

-- irritability /ɪrɪtəbˈɪləti/ *n.* 易怒、過敏性、興奮性

- **Irritability** can be found in some pregnant female animals since they have to protect their infants.

  在有些懷孕的雌性動物中能發現易怒的特徵，因為牠們要保護牠們的幼兒。

• KEY 166

-- repeatedly /rɪpˈitɪdli/ *adv.* 反復地、重復地

- Wasps can **repeatedly** sting the target, so they always prevail in the fight.

  黃蜂能重複性地螫目標，所以他們總是在戰鬥中獲取勝利。

• KEY 167

-- pleasure /plʼɛʒɚ/ *n.* 快樂、愉快、希望；*vt. vi.* （使）高興

- Whether the paralyzed tarantula gets the **pleasure** from the sting of the wasp is still debatable.

  被癱瘓的狼蛛是否從黃蜂的叮咬中獲取快樂仍是備受爭論的。

• KEY 168

-- detrimental /dˌɛtrəmʼɛntəl/ *adj.* 有害的

- Consumption of marine creatures on the top of the food chain can be quite **detrimental**.

  攝食在食物鏈頂端的海洋生物可能是有害的。

Unit 15 《劍 13》
Test 1 Reading Passage 3

Artificial Artists
人工藝術家

• KEY 169 ▶ MP3 15

-- possess /pəz'ɛs/ *vt.* 持有、佔有、使擁有、克制、支配、迷住

- Cao Ren **possesses** a secret weapon when he has a fight with Zhou Yu.

  當他與關羽對戰時，曹仁持有秘密武器。

• KEY 170

-- artificial /ˌɑrtəf'ɪʃəl/ *adj.* 人工的、人造的；矯揉造作的、不自然的

- **Artificial** trees are not quite suitable for the design of this restaurant.

  人工樹對於這間餐廳的設計來説不是那麼的合適。

• KEY 171

-- enrapture /ɛnr'æptʃɚ/ *vt.* 使狂喜

- An offer from Best Airlines **enraptures** Cindy, who has been dying to get in the industry for years.

收到倍斯特航空公司的錄取通知讓辛蒂欣喜若狂，她對於進入這個產業已經期盼數年。

• KEY 172

-- prestigious /prɛstˈɪdʒəs/ *adj.* 享有聲望的、聲望很高的

• Possessing a **prestigious** degree is not a guarantee to future success.

持有享譽盛名的學歷並不是未來成功的保證。

• KEY 173

-- sophisticated /səfˈɪstəkˌetɪd/ *adj.* 老練的、老於世故的；復雜的、尖端的

• A **sophisticated** look is a downside when you are a model.

當你是個模特兒時，老練的外貌是個缺點。

• KEY 174

-- exhibit /ɪgzˈɪbɪt/ *vt.* 展出、陳列；表示、顯出；*vi.* 開展覽會、展出產品展覽品、陳列品；顯示、呈現

• The model **exhibiting** a rare temperament of being a middle-aged aristocrat is what we are looking for.

模特兒所展現出罕見的中年貴族般氣質是我們所要的。

• KEY 175

-- mechanical /məkˈænɪkəl/ *adj.* 機械的、用機械的；機械學的；

機械似的、呆板的；手工操作的

- **Mechanical** gardens are extremely rare in an agricultural town.

機械式的花園在農村小鎮是相當罕見的。

• KEY 176

-- imagination /ɪm,ædʒən'eʃən/ *n.* 想象力；空想、妄想；想象出來的事物

- **Imagination** can be good for a job that constantly needs novel ideas.

想像力對於需要不斷有新奇想法的工作是個好事。

• KEY 177

-- objective /əbdʒ'ɛktɪv/ *adj.* 客觀的、外在的、受詞的

- You cannot expect an interview to be **objective** because it is evaluated by human beings.

你不能期待面試是客觀的因為是由人類所作的評估。

• KEY 178

-- reckon /r'ɛkən/ *vt.* 計算、總計、估計、認為、猜想；*vi.* 數、計算、估計、依賴、料想

- The special design of the orchard can **reckon** the number of birds visiting in a day.

果園特別的設計能夠估算出一天之內鳥類的拜訪次數。

• KEY 179

-- irresistible /ˌɪrɪz'ɪstəbəl/ *adj.* 不可抵抗的、不能壓制的

- An **irresistible** urge to eat is a great hindrance to lose weight.

  無法克制吃東西的衝動是減重的一大障礙。

• KEY 180

-- enjoyment /ɛndʒ'ɔɪmənt/ *n.* 享受、享有；歡樂、愉快；樂趣

- The **enjoyment** of eating ice cream is quite transient especially when the coldness fades away.

  吃冰淇淋的樂趣是相當短暫的，特別是當涼感消逝的時候。

Unit 16 《劍 13》
Test 2 Reading Passage 1

Bringing Cinnamon to Europe
將桂皮香料攜至歐洲

• KEY 181 ▶ MP3 16

-- fragrant /fr'egrənt/ *adj.* 芬香的、馥鬱的、愉快的

• Wild flowers make this place more **fragrant**, so lots of tourists love to linger there.

野花讓這個地方更芬芳了，所以許多觀光客喜愛停留在這兒。

• KEY 182

-- ingredient /ɪngr'idiənt/ *n.* 成分、因素

• The chef is not willing to share the key **ingredient** in public because it is a secret family recipe.

廚師不願意在大庭廣眾下分享關鍵成分，因為這是家庭秘密食譜。

• KEY 183

-- scent /s'ɛnt/ *n.* 氣味、香味、香水、蹤跡

• After kissing, the married man was unaware that the **scent** of the young lady left on his cloth.

在親吻後，已婚男子沒有察覺到年輕女士的香氣遺留在他的衣服上了。

• KEY 184

-- purchase /pˈɚtʃəs/ *vt.* 購買、贏得、努力取得、舉起

• To **purchase** the latest smartphone, Tom has to live a really frugal lifestyle so that he will have enough cash next month.

為了購買最新型的智慧型手機，湯姆真的必須要樽節度日，這樣他下個月才能有足夠的現金。

• KEY 185

-- consumption /kənsˈʌmpʃən/ *n.* 消費、消費量、憔悴

• **Consumption** of smartphones dwindled last week to only 5,000, shocking several shop owners.

上週智慧型手機的消費減至僅 5000 隻，震驚幾間店主。

• KEY 186

-- ailment /ˈelmənt/ *n.* 小病、疾病

• The **ailment** is pretty mild, so the doctor does not spend so much time talking to the patient.

疾病相當輕微，所以醫生不用花費很多時間在跟病患談論。

• KEY 187

-- indigestion /ˌɪndaɪdʒˈɛstʃən/ *n.* 消化不良

- People with a fragile stomach should be really careful when eating, otherwise, **indigestion** can happen very often.

  有脆弱的胃的人應該在吃東西時更加小心，否則消化不良會很常發生。

• KEY 188

-- transport /trænspˈɔrt/ *vt.* 傳送、運輸、流放

- **Transporting** fruits by using livestock is not as efficient as other means of transportation.

  藉由家畜運送水果並沒有其他運輸方式那麼有效率。

• KEY 189

-- exorbitant /ɪgzˈɔrbɪtənt/ *adj.* 過度的、過高的、過分的

- **Exorbitant** fishing can damage the local ecosystem, and that requires years to recover.

  過度捕撈會對當地生態系統造成損害，而這需要幾年來恢復。

• KEY 190

-- cultivation /kˌʌltɪvɪˈeʃən/ *n.* 耕作、栽培、培養

- **Cultivation** of the horseradish can be detrimental to the soil.

  耕種山葵可能對於土壤來説是有害的。

• KEY 191

-- harvest /hˈɑrvəst/ *n.* 收獲、成果、收獲物、收獲期；*vt. vi.* 收割、收獲

- The **harvest** of strawberries in this season is prolific, so the owner shares some with small animals.
  這季草莓的收穫量是多的，所以莓果主人分享一些給小動物。

• KEY 192

-- lucrative /lˈukrətɪv/ *adj.* 有利益的、獲利的、合算的

- The selling of strawberries is not as **lucrative** as it used to be.
  草莓的銷售沒有往常那樣利潤豐厚。

Unit 17 《劍 13》
Test 2 Reading Passage 2

Oxytocin
催產素

• KEY 193 ▶ MP3 17

-- hormone /hˈɔrm‚on/ *n.* 荷爾蒙

• Male **hormone** has driven numerous soldiers crazy, so nutritionists have tried to use several herbs in every meal.
男性賀爾蒙驅使許多軍人瘋狂，所以營養師們已經試著在每餐使用幾種藥草。

• KEY 194

-- prairie /prˈɛri/ *n.* 大草原、牧場

• The **prairie** is green in a way that you can hardly know the direction.
大草原油綠到你幾乎無法辨別方向。

• KEY 195

-- attachment /əˈtætʃmənt/ *n.* 附件、附屬物

• Females should not be the **attachment** of their husbands, and they should be financially independent.

女性不應該是她們丈夫的附屬品，而且她們應該要財務獨立。

• KEY 196

-- empathetic /ˌɛmpəˈθɛtɪk/ *adj.* 具同理心的

- Being **empathetic** is quite an essential trait for the person wanting to be a psychologist.

具有同理心是對於每個想要成為心理學家者相當重要的特質。

• KEY 197

-- emerge /ɪmˈɚdʒ/ *vi.* 浮現、形成、（由某種狀態）脫出、（事實）顯現出來

- A coffin suddenly **emerged** onto the surface of the river, shocking multiple visitors.

一副棺材突然浮現在河面上，震驚了許多拜訪者。

• KEY 198

-- invest /ɪnˈvɛst/ *vt.* 給...著衣；投資；*vi.* 投資；買進

- **Investing** more money only drags investors into the abysmal.

投資更多金錢僅把投資客拖進無底深淵。

• KEY 199

-- anonymous /ənˈɑnəməs/ *adj.* 作者不詳的、佚名的、無名的

- The author of the famous story prefers to remain

anonymous.

著名故事的作者偏好維持匿名身分。

• KEY 200

-- fuel /fjʼuəl/ *vt.* 加燃料、供以燃料；*vi.* 得到燃料

- The sudden announcement of the marriage **fuels** another one.

  突然的婚姻公告譜出另一個婚姻。

• KEY 201

-- disposition /dˌɪspəzʼɪʃən/ *n.* 處理、處置權；佈置、安排；性情、稟性、意向

- In this movie, actors are required to demonstrate more than ten types of **dispositions**, so it is quite challenging.

  在這電影裡，主角必須要分飾多於十個類別的性情，所以是相當有挑戰性的。

• KEY 202

-- subtlety /sʼʌtəlti/ *n.* 微妙、精明

- The **subtlety** of the martial arts skills can only be understood through years of deliberate practice.

  武功的精妙僅能透過數年的刻意練習來透徹理解。

• KEY 203

-- nuance /nʼuɑns/ *n.* 細微差別

- Only experienced farmers know the **nuance** between true herbs and fake ones.
  僅有有經驗的農夫知道真的草藥和仿冒版的細微差別。

· KEY 204

-- spotlight /sp'ɑtl,ɑɪt/ *n.* 聚光燈、探照燈;視聽、注意、醒目
- Cindy does not want to be a **spotlight**, but her job requires her to host major events.
  辛蒂不想要成為鎂光燈的焦點,但是她的工作需要她主持主要的活動。

Unit 18 《劍 13》
Test 2 Reading Passage 3

Making the Most of Trends
充分利用趨勢

• KEY 205 ▶ MP3 18

-- recognize /rˈɛkəgnˌaɪz/ *vt.* 認出、認可、承認、公認、賞識；
   vi. 具結

- The boss **recognizes** someone who is willing to admit the fault and later finds a way to correct it.
  老闆認可願意坦承錯誤且之後尋找方式改正的人。

• KEY 206

-- profound /profˈaʊnd/ *adj.* 極深的、深奧的、深厚的、深刻的、淵博的

- The martial arts skills are too **profound** for the beginner like John.
  武功對於像是約翰這樣的初學者來說太為深奧。

• KEY 207

-- jeopardize /dʒˈɛpəˌdˌaɪz/ *vt.* 危害、使受危困、使陷危地

- Introducing a non-native species **jeopardizes** the living of local animals.

引進外來種危害到當地動物的生活。

• KEY 208

-- cede /s'id/ *vt.* 放棄

- For male lions, **ceding** the ruling means losing a pride of lions.

對於雄性獅子來說，放棄統治意味著失去獅群。

• KEY 209

-- expansively /ɪks`pænsɪvlɪ/ *adv.* 可擴張地；廣闊地

- The picturesque valley is not as **expansively** as we expected.

風景如畫的山谷沒有我們預期的那樣廣闊。

• KEY 210

-- engender /ɛndʒ'ɛndɚ/ *vt.* 產生、引起；*vi.* 發生、形成

- The sudden arrival of Helen **engendered** the gossip from local residents.

海倫突然的到來引起當地人的八卦。

• KEY 211

-- retain /rɪt'en/ *vt.* 保持、保留；留住、擋住;記住

- **Retaining** a talented employee is arduous because he or she might have too many options.

留住有才能的員工是艱難的因為他或她可能有太多選擇。

• KEY 212

-- attribute /ˈætrəbjˈut/ *n.* 屬性

- HR managers are trying to find candidates who have the **attribute** of being really clever.

  人事經理正找真正具有聰明特質的候選人。

• KEY 213

-- unleash /ənˈiʃ/ *vt.* 解開...的皮帶、解除...的束縛、解放、釋放

- Loosening the rope on the horse **unleashes** the stress it suppresses in the body.

  鬆開馬身上的繩子解放了壓抑在其身上的壓力。

• KEY 214

-- opulence /ˈɑpjələns/ *n.* 豐裕、豐富、豐饒

- The wealth of the town rests on the **opulence** of sea creatures, such as lobsters and crabs.

  小鎮的財富仰賴海洋生物的富饒，例如龍蝦和螃蟹。

• KEY 215

-- mindset /mˈaɪndsˌɛt/ *n.* 心態、傾向、習慣

- The **mindset** is highly relevant to the success of one's career.

心態與一個人職涯的成功是高度相關的。

KEY 216

-- irrelevant /ɪˋrɛləvənt/ *adj.* 不恰當的、無關係的、不對題的

• **Irrelevant** topics can be helpful when team members cannot come up with a solution.

當團隊成員無法想出解決之道時，不相關的主題可能是有幫助的。

Unit 19 《劍 13》
Test 3 Reading Passage 1

The Coconut Palm
椰子樹

• KEY 217 ▶ MP3 19

-- envisage /ɛnvˈɪzɪdʒ/ *vt.* 面對、正視、想像

• The designer is trying to **envisage** the image of black bears that can be used in the jewelry design.
設計師正想像黑熊的圖相可能可以用於珠寶設計。

• KEY 218

-- slender /slˈɛndɚ/ *adj.* 纖細的、苗條的；微少的、微薄的

• Being **slender** has given Cindy many advantages, such as health and pursuers.
維持苗條身材已經給辛蒂許多優勢，例如擁有健康和追求者。

• KEY 219

-- endangered /ɪndˈendʒɚd/ *adj.* 瀕臨絕種的

• Certain types of scorpions are now **endangered**, so ecologists are educating local residents about the preservation of those creatures and the diversity of the ecosystem.

特定類型的毒蠍現今已經瀕臨絕種，所以生態學家正在教育當地居民關於那些生物的物種保存和生態系統的多樣性。

• KEY 220

-- surmount /sɚˈmaʊnt/ *vt.* 戰勝、超越、克服

- To **surmount** weather conditions, explorers have decided to stay in a nearby cave, waiting for the storm to go away.

為了克服天候狀況，探索者已經決定要待在鄰近的洞穴，等待風暴遠去。

• KEY 221

-- immature /ˌɪməˈtjʊr/ *adj.* 不成熟的、未完全發展的

- The lion cub is still too **immature** to realize the real menaces around him.

獅幼仍不夠成熟到能理解他周遭的真正威脅。

• KEY 222

-- weigh /weˈ/ *vt.* 稱…重量、衡量、重壓、考慮、權衡、起錨；*vi.* 稱分量、有意義、重壓

- The second interview **weighs** heavily on who gets hired and who does not.

第二次面試很大程度地權衡著誰獲得錄用和誰落選。

• KEY 223

-- derivative /də'ıvətıv/ *n.* 引出的、系出的引出之物、系出物、衍生字

- The fantastic dish is actually the **derivative** of a certain vegetable, according to a report.

  根據一則報導指出，美好的菜餚實際上是特定蔬菜的衍生物。

• KEY 224

-- maritime /m'ɛrət'ɑɪm/ *adj.* 海的、海上的、海事的、沿海的、海員的

- The crews applying for high-paying **maritime** positions require at least five years of experience.

  船員申請高薪的海事職位需要至少五年的經驗。

• KEY 225

-- viable /v'ɑɪəbəl/ *adj.* 能養活的、能生育的

- Whether golden dart frogs can be **viable** in artificial surroundings is still questionable.

  箭毒蛙是否能於人工環境中存活下來仍是備受質疑的。

• KEY 226

-- indefinitely /ınd'ɛfənətli/ *adv.* 不確定地

- Island lizards **indefinitely** roam on the shore, trying to escape predators and find the shelter.

  島上蜥蜴不確定地漫遊在岸邊，試圖逃避掠食者和找到庇護所。

🔑 KEY 227

-- germinate /dʒ'ə·mən、et/ *vi.* 發芽、萌芽、開始發育；*vt.* 使發
芽、使發達

- During this time, lots of plants are starting to **germinate** and grow.

  在這個時期，許多植物正在發芽和生長。

🔑 KEY 228

-- indigenous /ɪnd'ɪdʒənəs/ *adj.* 本土的、土著的、國產的

- **Indigenous** species can sometimes be threatened by non-native species.

  本土物種有時候可能會威脅到外來物種。

PART 1 雅思精選必考字彙

PART 2 實力檢測 Vocabulary in Context

Unit 20 《劍 13》
Test 3 Reading Passage 2

How Baby Talk Gives Infant Brains a Boost
嬰兒腔對幼兒大腦的促進

• KEY 229  ▶ MP3 20

-- exaggerate /ɪgz'ædʒɚ,et/ *vt.* 誇張、誇大；*vi.* 誇張、誇大
* The advertisement **exaggerates** the therapeutic effects of lung cancer.
  廣告誇大了肺癌的治療效果。

• KEY 230

-- repetitious /r'ɛpət'ɪʃəs/ *adj.* 多次反復的、重復的、反復性的
* After a **repetitious** attempt, the octopus eventually captures an exceedingly large lobster.
  在重複性的嘗試後，章魚最終捕抓到非常大隻的龍蝦。

• KEY 231

-- fascination /f,æsən'eʃən/ *n.* 魔力、入迷、魅力
* The **fascination** of the restaurant rests on freshness of the food and innovation.

餐廳的魔力仰賴食物的新鮮度和創新。

• KEY 232

-- exposure /ɪksp'oʒɚ/ n. 暴露、揭發、受到；曝光、輻照

- Long **exposure** to the sun can make clams cooked, so they have to remain underground.

  長時間曝曬在陽光下會讓牡蠣被煮熟了，所以牡蠣必須要留在地下。

• KEY 233

-- fundamental /fˌʌndəm'ɛntəl/ adj. 基礎的、基本的、十分重要的；n. 基本原則、基本原理

- Playing plays a **fundamental** role in how lions learn the movement, ambush, and hunting skills.

  獅子在玩耍中學習如何律動、埋伏和狩獵技巧上扮演基礎的角色。

• KEY 234

-- babble /b'æbəl/ vi. 呀呀學語、喋喋不休；vt. 嘮叨、吐露

- Infants learn how to speak by **babbling** words they hear around the environment.

  嬰兒藉由他們在周遭環境中聽到的字呀呀學語地學習如何說話。

• KEY 235

-- boost /b'ust/ n. vt. 推進、提高、捧場、促進

- Replicating the parents' way of flying, the young has a significant **boost** in his flying ability.

  複製父母的飛翔方式，幼鳥在牠的飛行能力上有著顯著的進步。

🔑 KEY 236

-- synthesize /s'ɪnθəsˌɑɪz/ *v.* 合成、綜合、綜合處理

- After **synthesizing** all the clues, the security eventually figures out who is the only suspect.

  在綜合所有線索後，保安人員最終了解到誰是嫌疑犯。

🔑 KEY 237

-- speculate /sp'ɛkjəl'et/ *vi.* 深思、推測、投機

- Female lions **speculate** that one of the missing cubs might get eaten by hyenas.

  雌性獅子推測到其中一隻失蹤的幼獸可能已經被土狼吃了。

🔑 KEY 238

-- slightly /sl'ɑɪtli/ *adv.* 輕微地

- During the chase, one of the female lions is **slightly** kicked by a giraffe, but remains unharmed.

  在追逐期間，其中一位雌性獅子被長頸鹿輕微地踢中，但是仍維持毫髮無傷。

🔑 KEY 239

-- prompt /pr'ɑmpt/ *v.* 促成

- Desperation for a guy has **prompted** her to seek a normal cottage boy.

  急迫找到男人已經促成了她找尋普通的農村男孩。

KEY 240

-- uncover /ənkˈʌvɚ/ *vt.* 揭露、揭開、暴露、脫⋯帽致敬；*vi.* 脫帽致敬、揭去蓋子

- Reporters **uncovered** more evidence about missing mammals in Africa, according to Best newspaper.

  根據倍斯特報紙，通訊員揭露更多關於非洲哺乳類動物失蹤的證據。

Unit 21 《劍 13》
Test 3 Reading Passage 3

Whatever Happened to the Harappan Civilisation
哈拉帕文明究竟發生了什麼事?

• KEY 241 ▶ MP3 21

-- depiction /dɪp'ɪkʃən/ *n.* 描寫、敘述

* **Depictions** of taboo topics have made bloggers popular.
  禁忌性的話題描述已經使得部落客們火紅。

• KEY 242

-- unclean /ənkl'in/ *adj.* 不潔淨的、不純潔的、行為不檢的

* The chef's **unclean** way of dealing with several dishes is so unsanitary.
  廚師不乾淨的處理幾道佳餚是如此不衛生的。

• KEY 243

-- exhaust /ɪgz'ɔst/ *vt.* 使筋疲力盡、耗盡;抽完、汲幹；*vi.* 排出氣體、被排出排氣、排出

* Three lions are trying to **exhaust** the strength of a small elephant.

三頭獅子正試圖耗盡小象的力氣。

• KEY 244

-- alter /ˈɔltɚ/ *vt.* 改變、更改、修改

- One of the lions unexpectedly **alters** the moving direction, astounding the prey.

  令人意想不到的是，其中一隻獅子更改了移動方向，讓獵物感到震驚。

• KEY 245

-- inhabit /ɪnhˈæbət/ *vt.* 居住於、占據、棲息

- Numerous octopuses **inhabit** the sea floor in the Pacific, making food resources rather scanty.

  許多的章魚居住在太平洋的海洋底層，讓食物資源相當貧乏。

• KEY 246

-- inaccuracy /ɪnˈækjɚəsi/ *n.* 不準確

- **Inaccuracy** of moving chequers on the chessboard makes them locked in an ancient tomb.

  不正確的移動棋盤上的棋子讓他們困在古墓裡頭。

• KEY 247

-- astonishing /əstˈɑnɪʃɪŋ/ *adj.* 令人驚訝、驚人的

- **Astonishing** numbers of antiques were found in an ancient tomb, making collectors thrilled.

PART 1 雅思精選必考字彙

PART 2 實力檢測 Vocabulary in Context

驚人數量的古董在古墓中被發現，這讓收藏家們感到興奮。

• KEY 248

-- definitive /dɪf'ɪnɪtɪv/ *adj.* 限定的、決定性的

- The **definitive** moment for an ostrich's life depends on the kick to the abdomen of the cheetah.
鴕鳥性命的決定性的時刻仰賴於踢在獵豹腹部的一擊。

• KEY 249

-- exceed /ɪks'id/ *vt.* 超過、勝過；越出；*vi.* 超過其他、突出

- The male ostrich ultimately **exceeds** his rival winning the heart of the female ostrich.
雄性鴕鳥最終超過了他的敵手贏得雌性鴕鳥的芳心。

• KEY 250

-- weaken /w'ikən/ *vt.* 削弱、減弱、使稀薄；*vi.* 變弱、變軟弱

- Antitoxin **weakens** venom circulating in blood vessels.
抗毒素弱化了循環在血管中的毒素。

• KEY 251

-- combination /k,ɑmbən'eʃən/ *n.* 合併；組合

- A **combination** of both naval and air forces is the key of winning the battle.
海上和空中軍力的結合是贏得戰鬥的主要關鍵。

• KEY 252

-- distinctive /dɪst'ɪŋktɪv/ *adj.* 區別性的、鑑別性的、有特色的、特別的

- Zebras are known for their **distinctive** stripes, whereas giraffes are noted for their long necks.

  斑馬以牠們具特色的斑紋而聞名,而長頸鹿以牠們的長脖子為人所知。

Unit 22 《劍 13》
Test 4 Reading Passage 1

Cutty Sark: the Fastest Sailing Ship of all Time
卡提沙克號：史上最快的帆船

• KEY 253 ▸ MP3 22

-- vessel /v'ɛsəl/ *n.* 船隻；容器、器皿；血管、導管

- **Vessels** are sailing at an exceedingly great speed so that fishermen can catch up with the last harvest.

  船隻正以極快的速度行駛，這樣一來漁夫們就能捕獲最後一次的捕撈。

• KEY 254

-- dominate /d'ɑmən,et/ *vt. vi.* 支配、占優勢

- Even though crocodiles are **dominating** the swamp and nearby river, pythons do pose a great threat to them.

  即使鱷魚在沼澤和鄰近的溪邊佔優勢，巨蟒對牠們造成很大程度的威脅。

• KEY 255

-- laden /l'edən/ *adj.* 充滿的、負載的、苦惱的

- The colossal ship is **laden** with gold and silver, making it a target for pirates.

  巨型船艦載負著金和銀，讓它成了海盜的目標。

• KEY 256

-- misfortune /mɪsfˈɔrtʃən/ *n.* 不幸、災禍、壞運氣

- The **misfortune** of the crocodile is to get targeted by an agile cheetah.

  鱷魚的不幸是被靈巧的獵豹鎖定目標。

• KEY 257

-- daunting /dˈɔntɪŋ/ *adj.* 使人畏縮的

- The **daunting** task is designed to frighten most newly recruits.

  令人畏縮的任務是設計用來嚇唬大多數的新聘員工。

• KEY 258

-- succeed /səksˈid/ *vi.* 成功；繼續、繼承；*vt.* 繼…之後、接著…發生

- The young prince **succeeded** the throne and inherited an enormous amount of wealth.

  年輕王子繼承了王位而且繼承了巨大的財富。

• KEY 259

-- replacement /rɪplˈesmənt/ *n.* 替換、代替；代替的人

- The CEO of Best Airlines has been seeking for a **replacement** for months, but cannot seem to find one.
倍斯特航空的 CEO 已經嘗試尋找接替人員數個月了，但是卻無法找到合適的人。

• KEY 260

-- incompetent /ɪnkˈɑmpətənt/ *adj.* 無能力的、無力的、不適當的；*n.* 不勝任的無能力者
- The CEO cannot tolerate **incompetent** employees, so layoffs are actually a common scene in the company.
- CEO 無法忍受沒有能力的員工，所以解雇實際上是公司中司空見慣的事。

• KEY 261

-- suspend /səspˈɛnd/ *vt.* 懸、吊、使懸浮、暫停、中止、推遲；
vi. 暫停、中止、懸浮、宣佈破產
- The male lion had a slip and got **suspended** under the bridge.
雄性獅子滑了一步且懸吊在橋下。

• KEY 262

-- hemisphere /hˈɛmɪsf,ɪr/ *n.* 半球、地球的半面、大腦半球
- You cannot find wild koalas in the northern **hemisphere** because they are native to Australia.
你無法在北半球找到野生無尾熊因為牠們原產於澳洲。

KEY 263

-- miscellaneous /mˌɪsəl'eniəs/ *adj.* 各種的、多方面的

- Rainforests contain **miscellaneous** creatures, and some even have medicinal qualities.

  熱帶雨林包含多樣的生物，而有些甚至有醫療特質。

KEY 264

-- continue /kənt'ɪnju/ *vi.* 繼續、延續、延長；*vt.* 使繼續、使延長

- Surprisingly, the price of gold **continued** to climb, eventually reaching the climax of around 1500 dollars per gram.

  令人感到意外的是，金子的價格持續攀升，最終達到每公克大約 1500 元的高點。

Unit 23 《劍 13》
Test 4 Reading Passage 2

Saving the Soil
拯救土壤

• KEY 265 ▶ MP3 23

-- farmable /fˈɑrmˈebəl/ *adj.* 能夠耕種的

• The nearby land contains rich soil, so it is deemed as quite **farmable** to eyes of farmers.
  鄰近的土地包含富饒的土壤，所以在農夫眼中被視為是相當能夠耕種的。

• KEY 266

-- degradation /dˌɛɡrədˈeʃən/ *n.* 降格、墮落、退化

• The **degradation** of the land makes it not profitable and valueless.
  土壤的退化讓其不具利益用處且沒有價值。

• KEY 267

-- researcher /rˈisətʃə/ *n.* 研究員；調查者

• To analyse the behavior of brown bears, **researchers** have decided to set up high-tech cameras in the valley so that they can have more solid evidence.

為了分析棕熊的行為，研究人員們已經決定要在山谷內架設高科技攝影機，這樣一來他們就能夠有更多實質證據。

🔑 KEY 268

-- decompose /d,ikəmp'oz/ *vt. vi.* 分解、（使）腐爛

- Bacteria eventually **decompose** rotten fruits on the forest floor.

  細菌最終分解了森林底部腐敗的水果。

🔑 KEY 269

-- atmosphere /'ætməsf`ɪr/ *n.* 大氣、空氣、氣氛、大氣層、大氣圈

- The **atmosphere** in the coffee shop is romantic and dreamy, so people are willing to spend hundreds of dollars for a cup of coffee.

  咖啡店的氣氛是浪漫且夢幻的，所以人們願意花費數百元在一杯咖啡上。

🔑 KEY 270

-- property /pr'ɑpəti/ *n.* 財產、資產、地產；財產權、所有權；性質、性能

- The **property** of the valley is belonged to a wealthy merchant.

山谷的所有權是屬於富有的商人的。

🔑 KEY 271

-- uncultivated /'ʌnk'ʌltəv,etəd/ *adj.* 不文明的、無教養的

- **Uncultivated** herbs might be rather invaluable, so considerable farmers are considering raising them in the following season.

  無耕種的藥草可能相當價值連城，所以相當多的農夫正考慮要在下季耕植它們。

🔑 KEY 272

-- inconvenient /,ɪnkənv'injənt/ *adj.* 不便的、有困難的

- The cliff-like geography makes distribution of supplies rather **inconvenient** and challenging.

  峭壁般的地理讓供給的分布相當不便且具挑戰性。

🔑 KEY 273

-- indiscriminate /ɪndɪskr'ɪmənət/ *adj.* 無差別的、不分皂白的、雜陳的

- An **indiscriminate** accuse was made in the court yesterday, and the jury might believe the accuse brought up by the prosecutor.

  昨日法庭中有著不分青紅皂白的控訴，而陪審團可能相信由檢控官所提起的控訴。

KEY 274

-- overuse /ˌovɚˈjuz/ *vt.* 使用過度過度使用、任意驅使

- The land has been **overused**, so it will take years to recover to the cultivated, fertile land.

  土地已經過度使用，所以將會需要幾年的時間恢復成可耕作且豐饒的土地。

KEY 275

-- assess /əsˈɛs/ *vt.* 評價、評估、評判、評定；徵收、課

- The female impala is still **assessing** whether the male is qualified enough to mate her or not.

  雌性黑斑羚正評估雄性是否足以符合跟她交配的資格。

KEY 276

-- accessible /æksˈɛsəbəl/ *adj.* 易於得到的、易於進入的、可處理的、可存取的

- Fruits are abundant on every tree; thus, they are easily **accessible** for small insects and larger birds.

  在每棵樹上，水果都豐碩，因此，它們更易被小型昆蟲和較大型的鳥類取用。

Book Review
書籍評論

• KEY 277 ▶ MP3 24

-- external /ɪkst'ə·nəl/ *adj.* 外部的、客觀的、表面的

- We cannot rely on **external** incentives to motivate us to learn because it will not last long.

  我們無法仰賴外部誘因驅策我們學習，因為這樣並不持久。

• KEY 278

-- summarize /s'ʌmə,ɑɪz/ *vt. vi.* 概述、總結、摘要而言

- The rookie is asked to **summarize** the whole PPT presentation on the first day at work.

  菜鳥在第一天上班時就被要求要摘要全部的簡報。

• KEY 279

-- oblivious /əbl'ɪviəs/ *adj.* 忘卻的、忘記的、健忘的、不注意的

- Some predators are **oblivious** and cannot recall the stashed meat hidden earlier.

有些掠食者是健忘的且無法回想出稍早前儲藏的肉在哪裡。

• KEY 280

-- reconcile /rˈɛkəns,ɑɪl/ *vt.* 使和解、調停、使和諧、使一致、使順從、使聽從

* To **reconcile** the fight between two brothers, mother bears handed in a huge slice of honey to them, footage never before seen in years.

為了調停兩兄弟間的紛爭，母熊遞了一大片蜂蜜給牠們，這是幾年內未見過的視頻。

• KEY 281

-- pursuit /pɚˈsˈut/ *n.* 追蹤、追捕、追求、追趕、工作、職業

* The **pursuit** of wealth has turned Tom into a greedy and ruthless man.

追求財富已經使得湯姆轉變成貪婪且殘暴的男人。

• KEY 282

-- illiterate /ɪlˈɪtɚət/ *adj.* 目不識丁的、沒受教育的

* **illiterate** kids are peculiar in the town because going to school will not cost a cent from this year.

在小鎮裡頭，沒受過教育的小孩是罕見的，因為今年上學不會花費到一分錢。

🔑 KEY 283

-- entirety /ɪntˈɑɪɚti/ *n.* 全面、全部、全體、完全

• The **entirety** of the strawberries in the warehouse was stolen by experienced employees who are desperate for money.

在倉庫裡頭全部的草莓都被急切用錢的有經驗員工給偷走了。

🔑 KEY 284

-- unforgeable /ˈʌnfˈɔrdʒ əb!/ *adj.* 不可鍛造的

• The broken sword is **unforgeable** unless the temperature reaches at least 3,000 Celsius.

斷裂的劍是不可鍛造的，除非溫度達到至少攝氏 3000 度。

🔑 KEY 285

-- pleasurable /plˈɛʒɚəbəl/ *adj.* 快樂的、愉快的、心情舒暢的

• After consuming ten giant mantises, the female chameleon feels **pleasurable** and maintains quite friendly towards other male chameleons.

在食用 10 隻大型螳螂後，雌性變色龍感到心情舒暢，對於其他雄性變色龍維持相當友好的態度。

🔑 KEY 286

-- sensation /sɛnsˈeʃən/ *n.* 感覺、感情、感動

• The female tiger has a strange **sensation** towards the latest arrival.

雌性老虎對於新來的訪客有著奇怪的感覺。

• KEY 287

-- displeasure /dɪspl'ɛʒɚ/ *n.* 不快、不滿、生氣

• The appearance of chameleons turning red can be the demonstration of their **displeasure**.

變色龍的外表轉變成紅色可能是在展示牠們的不快。

• KEY 288

-- desirable /dɪz'ɑɪrəbəl/ *adj.* 稱心的、中意的、理想的、希望的

• The male impala has found a **desirable** mate, but is get tested by her.

黑斑羚已經找到中意的伴侶，但卻要接受她的考驗。

Unit 25 《劍 12》
Test 1 Reading Passage 1

Cork
木栓

• KEY 289 ▶ MP3 25

-- remarkable /rɪmˈɑrkəbəl/ *adj.* 異常的、非凡的、顯著的；值得注意的

• Also **remarkable** is the fact that visitors are witnessing ostriches hatching their eggs in the wild Africa.
也值得注意的是，在野地非洲，拜訪者正目睹鴕鳥孵化牠們的蛋。

• KEY 290

-- buoyant /bˈɔɪənt/ *adj.* 有浮力的、心情愉快的

• The particular lizard is quite **buoyant**, so it can swim nearly the surface of the water.
那特別的蜥蜴相當的有浮力，所以牠幾乎能夠游在水的表面上。

• KEY 291

-- extraordinary /ɪkstrˈɔrdənˌɛri/ *adj.* 非常的、特別的、非凡的

- Getting stung by malicious scorpions was an **extraordinary** experience in an African trip.

  被惡毒的毒蠍螫到是這趟非洲之旅的獨特體驗。

• KEY 292

-- insulate /'ɪnsəl,et/ *vt.* 使絕緣、隔離

- Four tiger siblings are trying to **insulate** deer from its population.

  四隻老虎兄弟姊妹正試圖將鹿從其族群中隔離出來。

• KEY 293

-- constant /k'ɑnstənt/ *adj.* 不變的、一定的、時常的

- The hierarchy in the pride of lions remains pretty **constant**.

  獅群的階層維持相當的恆定。

• KEY 294

-- replicate /r'ɛplək,et/ *v.* 摺疊；複製

- To **replicate** the experience of elder elephants, younger elephants now know how to select better meals.

  為了複製年長象的體驗，年輕大象現在知道要如何選擇較佳的餐點。

• KEY 295

-- flourish /fl'ɝɪʃ/ *vi.* 繁榮、茂盛、活躍、手舞足蹈；*vt.* 揮舞、誇耀茂盛、興旺、華飾

- It is quite soothing to see all mushrooms **flourish** at the same time.

  看到蘑菇在同個時間繁盛是相當撫慰人心的。

-- moisture /mˈɔɪtʃɚ/ *n.* 濕氣、水分、降雨

- In the early morning, desert snakes are busy licking **moisture** or dew surrounded around the surface of their skin.

  在早晨，沙漠蛇正忙於舔著在牠們皮膚表面所圍繞著的溼氣或露水。

-- profession /prəfˈɛʃən/ *n.* 職業、表白、聲明、公開宣佈

- The **profession** of the doctor is still considered very noble.

  醫生的職業仍被視為是非常高尚的。

-- remainder /rɪmˈendɚ/ *n.* 剩餘物、其他的人、殘余、餘數

- The **remainder** of hyenas is so scared about the ensuing attack by four muscular male lions.

  殘餘的土狼如此懼怕四隻肌肉健壯的獅子接踵而來的攻擊。

-- monopoly /mənˈɑpəli/ *n.* 壟斷、專賣權、獨占事業

- The **monopoly** of the silver transport has led to several bloodshed.

  銀運輸的壟斷已經導致幾個流血衝突了。

• KEY 300

-- compound /kˈɑmpaʊnd/ *n.* 混合物、復合字、院子、復方、有圍牆的建築群

- The **compound** is actually the mixture of oil, soy sauce, and vinegar.

  這個混合物是油、醬油和醋的混合。

Unit 26《劍 12》
Test 1 Reading Passage 2

Collecting as a Hobby
將收藏當作嗜好

• KEY 301 MP3 26

-- fascinating /f'æsən'etɪŋ/ *adj.* 迷人的、吸引人的、使人神魂顛倒的

- The story is so **fascinating** that kids linger there even after it is finished.
  故事是如此吸引人以至於即使結束後，小孩仍在那流連忘返。

• KEY 302

-- dignify /d'ɪgnəf,ɑɪ/ *vt.* 增威嚴、使高貴、故做顯貴

- The merchant's house is **dignified** by two huge paintings and expensive antiques.
  商人的房子因為兩幅巨型的畫和昂貴的古董而顯得高貴。

• KEY 303

-- amass /əm'æs/ *vt.* 收集、積聚

- The young man has **amassed** enough wealth and ready to

propose to his girlfriend.

年輕男子已經累積了足夠的財富而且準備要向他女朋友求婚了。

• KEY 304

-- productive /prəd'ʌktɪv/ *adj.* 能生產的、有生產價值的、多產的

- The young writer is very **productive**, writing 10 articles in only a few hours.

  年輕作家非常多產，在幾小時內撰寫了 10 篇文章。

• KEY 305

-- triumph /tr'ɑɪəmf/ *n.* 勝利、成功；*vi.* 勝利、成功；狂歡、喜悅

- The **triumph** of outselling other companies did not last long and the figure was soon caught up in a few hours.

  在銷售上勝過其他公司的成功並沒有維持太久，而在幾小時內數值就被追上了。

• KEY 306

-- exchange /ɪkstʃ'endʒ/ *vt.* 交換、調換、兌換；交流、交易；*vi.* 交換、兌換;調換崗位或任務交換、調換

- **Exchanging** the role in a company is very common nowadays, so you need to be very adaptive.

  在公司調換職務在現今是非常常見的事，所以你需要非常有適應力。

PART 1 雅思精選必考字彙

PART 2 實力檢測 Vocabulary in Context

•KEY 307

-- purpose /pˈɚpəs/ *n.* 目的、意向、決心、效果、意義

- The **purpose** of writing this article is to inform lots of people that whaling is a bad thing.

  寫作這篇文章的目的是告知許多朋友獵捕鯨魚是件壞事。

•KEY 308

-- celebrate /sˈɛləbrˌet/ *vt. vi.* 慶祝、祝賀、舉行

- To **celebrate** the successful hunting for a giant elephant, several male lions roar for several minutes, claiming their status and power.

  為了慶祝成功的獵捕巨型象，幾隻雄性獅子咆嘯了幾分鐘，宣示牠們的地位和權力。

•KEY 309

-- inferior /ɪnfˈɪriɚ/ *adj.* 次等的、較低的、下方的

- **Inferior** qualities of wine will not be served on the dinner table because people will notice.

  較劣質的酒不會供應於晚餐餐桌上，因為人們會注意到。

•KEY 310

-- knowledgeable /nˈɑlədʒəbəl/ *adj.* 聰明的、有知識的

- The head of the female lion is very **knowledgeable**, so the hunt led by her often succeeds.

  雌性獅子的首領是非常有知識的，所以由牠帶頭的獵捕通常都會

成功。

KEY 311

-- notion /nˈoʃən/ *n.* 概念、觀念、想法、打算、主張

- The **notion** of adding vegetables in a chicken soup is not novel.

  添加蔬菜於雞湯裡頭的觀念並不是很新奇。

KEY 312

-- insecurity /ˌɪnsɪkjˈʊrɪti/ *n.* 不安全、不安全感

- A sense of **insecurity** permeates among female lions because they sense the smell of other male intruders.

  不安全感蔓延在雌性獅子中，因為牠們感受到其他雄性闖入者的氣味。

Unit 27 《劍 12》
Test 1 Reading Passage 3

What Is the Purpose of Gaining Knowledge?
獲取知識的目的是什麼呢?

• KEY 313 ▶ MP3 27

-- institution /ˌɪnstɪtˈuʃən/ *n.* 建立、設立【U】；公共機構【C】

- The **institution** was erected to enhance the spread of education.

  公共機構的設立是為了要增進教育的傳播。

• KEY 314

-- instruction /ɪnstrˈʌkʃən/ *n.* 教育【U】；教訓、教誨【U】；指示、命令

- The **instruction** given by the master was unclear, so disciples were not able to do the correct move.

  這位大師給予的指示是模糊的，所以門徒們不能夠做出正確的動作。

• KEY 315

-- career /kəˈɪr/ *n.* 經歷、生涯；專業、職業

PART 1 雅思精選必考字彙

PART 2 實力檢測 Vocabulary in Context

- The **career** is long, so you have to look for a long-term rather than a short term.

  職涯是長久的，所以你必須要看長遠而非短期。

• KEY 316

-- undergraduate /ˌʌndə·gr'ædʒəwət/ *n.* 大學生、大學肄業生

- **Undergraduates** really need to learn how to write a great resume before they graduate.

  在畢業前，大學生真的需要知道要如何撰寫出色的履歷。

• KEY 317

-- academic /ˌækəd'ɛmɪk/ *adj.* 專科院校的、研究院的、學會的；學術的、理論的

- **Academic** success is not a guarantee to the future success.

  學術成就不是未來成功的保證。

• KEY 318

-- intend /ɪnt'ɛnd/ *vt.* 想要、打算；打算使⋯為；意指、意思是

- Initially, he **intended** to file for a divorce, but did not do it, fearing that it could jeopardize his public image.

  起初，他意圖提起離婚訴訟，但最終沒有這麼做，因為害怕此舉會危及他的大眾印象。

• KEY 319

-- detect /dɪt'ɛkt/ *vt.* 察覺、發覺；偵查、探測；對⋯檢波

- Farm owners has **detected** visitors might have an agenda to their cellar.

農場主人已經察覺到拜訪者可能對他們的地窖有不軌的意圖。

• KEY 320

-- effective /ɪf'ɛktɪv/ *adj.* 有效的、有力的、實際的有生力量

- To make the poison **effective**, the wine should be kept warm enough so that toxin will not distill.

為了讓此毒生效，酒應該要保存在夠溫暖的地方，這樣一來毒性就不會被蒸餾掉。

• KEY 321

-- prosecution /pr,ɑsəkj'uʃən/ *n.* 實行、經營、起訴

- The **prosecution** astounded numerous buyers who claimed that they did not know the source was illegal.

起訴震驚了許多不知道其來源是非法的買家。

• KEY 322

-- principle /pr'ɪnsəpəl/ *n.* 原理、原則【C】；道義、德行

- The **principle** rests on the tide and the buoyancy of the water, so it is entirely feasible.

這個原理仰賴潮汐和水的浮力，所以這樣是全然可行的。

• KEY 323

-- expertise /,ɛkspɚt'iz/ *n.* 專家的意見、專門技術

- The consideration of exploding the tunnel requires **expertise** so that the damage can be minimized.

爆炸隧道的考量需要專家的意見，如此一來可以將損害降至最低。

• KEY 324

-- criminal /krˈɪmənəl/ *n.* 罪犯、犯人、刑事

- **Criminals** in this country are not allowed to have a visit with family members.

這個國家的罪犯的家庭成員沒有探視權。

Unit 28 《劍 12》
Test 2 Reading Passage 1

The Risks Agriculture Faces in Developing Countries
發展中國家的農業所面臨到的風險

• KEY 325 ▶ MP3 28

-- distinguish /dɪst'ɪŋgwɪʃ/ *vt.* 區別、辯明、識別；辨認出；*vi.* 區別、辨別、識別

- **Distinguishing** a fake jewelry requires high-tech equipment.
  辨別出仿冒的珠寶需要高科技的設備。

• KEY 326

-- production /prəd'ʌkʃən/ *n.* 生產【U】；產量【U】；產品、作品【C】

- The **production** of watermelons cannot meet with the demand, so the price goes up.
  西瓜的產量無法達到需求，所以價格上揚。

• KEY 327

-- adverse /ædv'ɚs/ *adj.* 不利的、敵對的、相反的、逆的

- Closure of ten huge companies in a month has an **adverse** effect on the economy.

在一個月內，十間大公司的倒閉對於經濟有負面的影響。

🔑 KEY 328

-- underlying /ˌʌndɚˈlɑɪɪŋ/ *adj.* 在下面的、潛在的

- The **underlying** assets should be distributed 70/30 between my client and his husband.

潛在的資產應該要以 **70/30** 比例分配給我的客戶和他的丈夫。

🔑 KEY 329

-- inability /ˌɪnəbˈɪlɪti/ *n.* 無能、無力

- His **inability** to compete with a higher offer during a bidding war led to a blame from the boss.

他無法在競價戰中與較高的喊價競爭導致他受到老闆的責備。

🔑 KEY 330

-- sufficient /səfˈɪʃənt/ *adj.* 足夠的、充分的

- **Sufficient** nutrients are what the children need the most.

足夠的營養素是小孩最需要的部分。

🔑 KEY 331

-- mitigate /mˈɪtəɡ,et/ *vt.* 鎮靜、緩和、減輕

- The traditional herb has miraculously **mitigated** his pain, but venom still roams in blood vessels.

傳統的草藥已經奇蹟似地減輕了他的痛，但是毒素仍舊蔓延在他

的血管中。

KEY 332

-- significantly /sɪgnˈɪfɪkəntli/ *adv.* 在相當大的程度上

- Sales bonuses have been **significantly** slashed due to the policy of the new CEO.
由於新 CEO 的政策，銷售獎金已經遭到大幅刪減。

KEY 333

-- reduce /rədˈus/ *vt.* 減少、分解、降低、使變為、把…分解、把…歸納；*vi.* 減少、變瘦

- To **reduce** the amount of chemical substance, we should use natural predators to control the number of pests.
為了減低化學物質的量，我們應該要使用天敵去控制害蟲的數量。

KEY 334

-- alleviate /əlˈivi,et/ *vt.* 減輕、使緩和

- Licking the wound of the cub is considered the comfort towards the young, **alleviating** the pain to some extent.
舔幼獸的傷口被視為是對年輕幼獸的撫慰，減輕某種程度的痛楚。

KEY 335

-- transfer /trænsfˈɚ/ *v.* 遷移、移動、傳遞、轉讓、轉移、匯兌；

vt. 轉移、調轉、調任、改變、傳遞

- Making a wire **transfer** is not that difficult, so you should give it a try.

  電匯不是那麼困難,所以你應該要試試看。

• KEY 336

-- resilient /rɪzˈɪljənt/ *adj.* 彈回的、有彈力的、愉快的

- People with a **resilient** mindset get bounced back really soon, so everyone should try to learn that.

  具彈性心態的人很快就回復了,所以每個人都應該要學習。

Unit 29 《劍 12》
Test 2 Reading Passage 2

The Lost City
失落的城市

KEY 337 🔘 ▶ MP3 29

-- achievement /ətʃ'ivmənt/ *n.* 完成、達到；成就、成績

• The **achievement** of earning one million dollars is highly likely for someone like Tom, who earns a lot.
  賺取一百萬元的成就對於像是湯姆那樣賺很多的人來說是非常有可能的。

KEY 338

-- exploration /,ɛksplə'eʃən/ *n.* 探險、踏勘、探測

• The female lion is doing the **exploration** for their newfound shelter.
  雌性獅子正在探索新找到的庇護所。

KEY 339

-- remains /rɪm'enz/ *n.* 剩餘物、廢墟、殘餘

• They could not find **remains** in the coffin, deducing that someone had come here earlier and took it away.

他們無法找到棺材裏頭的剩餘物，推論有人已經更早於他們到此並將它拿走了。

• KEY 340

-- advantage /ædv'æntɪdʒ/ *n.* 長處、好處、優點、優勢、利益、有利條件

* The **advantage** of living in the house is that you do not have to pay the rent.
生活在這間房子的優點是你不需要付房租。

• KEY 341

-- substantial /səbst'æntʃəl/ *adj.* 實質上的、物質的、有內容的、結實的

* The bonuses for executing this task is **substantial**, but no one volunteered in the first place.
執行這項任務的獎金很豐碩，但是沒有人在最初的時候自告奮勇。

• KEY 342

-- arrange /ɚ'endʒ/ *vt.* 整理、分類、排列；籌備、佈置、安排；*vi.* 安排；商定

* **Arranging** ten different manufacturers to meet in a day is difficult.
一天之內要安排 10 個不同的製造商碰面是困難的。

• KEY 343

-- accompany /ək'ʌmpəni/ *vt.* 伴隨、陪伴、陪同、伴奏、為…伴奏

- In the very end of every episode, the ending part always **accompanies** bloopers.

  在每季最後頭,結尾的部份總是伴隨著「洋相」。

• KEY 344

-- expectation /ˌɛkspɛkt'eʃən/ *n.* 期待、期望、指望、預料

- Parents all have a high **expectation** towards kids, making them stressful.

  父母對於小孩子都有很高的期望,讓小孩感到很大的壓力。

• KEY 345

-- considerable /kəns'ɪdəˈəbəl/ *adj.* 相當的、可觀的、重要的

- **Considerable** buffalos are trying to cross the river, making the scene quite remarkable.

  可觀的野牛正試圖穿過河,這個場景相當驚人。

• KEY 346

-- monumental /mˌɑnjəm'ɛntəl/ *adj.* 紀念碑的、做為紀念的、不朽的

- After discussing with one another, attorneys are worried that a **monumental** mistake could be made and wrong the accused.

在彼此討論過後，律師們擔憂可能會因為誤會被告，而犯下重大的錯誤。

• KEY 347

-- hindsight /h'aɪnds,aɪt/ *v.* 槍的照尺、後見之明

- With the benefit of the **hindsight**, the bank manager was making the right decision, and he should not get fired in the first place.

  有著後見之明的益處，銀行經理做了正確的決定，而且他不應該在起初就被解雇。

• KEY 348

-- abandon /əb'ændən/ *vt.* 拋棄、離棄、遺棄；放棄

- Female lions are **abandoning** the weak cub because in fact only very few healthy ones will make it to adulthood.

  雌性獅子正放棄弱的幼獸，因為實際上只有非常少的健康幼獸能活到成年。

Unit 30 《劍 12》
Test 2 Reading Passage 3

The Benefits of Being Bilingual
雙語的優勢

• KEY 349 ▶ MP3 30

-- population/p,ɑpjəl'eʃən/ *n.* 人口、人口數

• The **population** of sharks has decreased over the years due to rampant hunting activities.
由於猖獗的盜獵活動，鯊魚的族群已經在這幾年間減少了。

• KEY 350

-- disadvantage /d,ɪsədv'æntɪdʒ/ *n.*不利、不利條件【C】；損失、損害【U】

• The **disadvantage** of raising dogs is that they will jump at you when you come home.
眷養狗的缺點是每當你回到家時，牠們會躍向你。

• KEY 351

-- cognitive /k'ɑgnɪtɪv/ *adj.* 認知的、認識的、有認識力的

• **Cognitive** developments for kids are very important, so parents should seize the moment.

認知的發展對於小孩來説是非常重要的，所以父母應該要抓住時機。

• KEY 352

-- sequential /səkw'ɛntʃəl/ *adj.* 繼續的、後果的、連續的

- Not putting all toys in a **sequential** order, the boy gets punished by not getting ice cream.

因為沒有將所有玩具依序排列，小男孩被懲罰沒有冰淇淋。

• KEY 353

-- activate /'æktəv,et/ *vt.* 刺激、使活動、創設

- You need 80 digit numbers to **activate** the registration of the game.

你需要 80 個數位號碼來激活遊戲的註冊。

• KEY 354

-- corresponding /k,ɔrəsp'ɑndɪŋ/ *adj.* 符合的、一致的；通訊的

- Scientists have the **corresponding** prediction that the octopus will return to the same shelter, evading the attack by a flounder.

科學家們有著一致性的預測，章魚回到相同的庇護所，以逃避比目魚的攻擊。

• KEY 355

-- compelling /kəmp'ɛlɪŋ/ *adj.* 強制的、強迫性的、令人注目的

- The **compelling** move blocked attacks in different directions, making killers astounded.

引人注目的動作擋下了從不同方位而來的攻擊，讓殺手們感到震驚。

• KEY 356

-- persistent /pɚs'ɪstənt/ *adj.* 固執的、堅持的、持續的

- Mother polar bear's **persistent** search for the carcasses eventually paid off.

雌性北極熊持之以恆的找尋屍體最終有所收穫。

• KEY 357

-- juggle /dʒ'ʌgəl/ *vi.* 玩戲法、行騙、篡改；*vt.* 耍弄、歪曲、篡改
玩戲法、魔術、欺騙

- **Juggling** between family and career can make someone exhausted and aged.

在家庭和職涯中取得平衡可能讓一個人感到筋疲力竭和年華盡失。

• KEY 358

-- perceptual /pɚs'ɛptʃəwəl/ *adj.* 知覺的、有知覺的

- Dolphins are keenly **perceptual**, so they are more intelligent than some mammals.

海豚是具有敏銳性知覺的,所以牠們比起一些哺乳類動物更聰明。

• KEY 359

-- categorize /k'ætəgə‚ɑɪz/ *vt.* 分類、歸類

- **Categorizing** similar colors should not be very difficult for a fashion editor.

將相似的顏色分類對於時尚編輯來說應該不是太困難。

• KEY 360

-- symptom /s'ɪmptəm/ *n.* 症狀、徵候、徵兆

- People with this kind of **symptom** are often in the stage 3 of lung cancer.

有這樣徵狀的人通常是到了肺癌第三期。

Unit 31 《劍 12》
Test 7 Reading Passage 1

Flying Tortoises
「放飛」烏龜

• KEY 361 MP3 31

-- uneven /ən'ivən/ *adj.* 不平均的、不均勻的、奇數的

- **Uneven** distributions of tree seeds in the area make this place look like a labyrinth.

  這個地區樹的種子分布不均勻造成此地看起來像是個迷宮。

• KEY 362

-- separate /s'ɛpə,et/ *v.* 分離；分隔

- Mother polar bear and her babies are **separated** by ice floes.

  母北極熊和她的小孩被大浮冰分隔開來了。

• KEY 363

-- distinct /dɪst'ɪŋkt/ *adj.* 清楚的、明顯的；截然不同的、獨特的

- His **distinct** way of using the sword somehow balances the weakness detected by foes.

他獨特運劍的方式不知如何地平衡掉了敵人察覺到的劣勢。

🔑 KEY 364

-- resemble /rɪz'ɛmbəl/ *vt.* 相似、類似、像

● His leaping resembles certain sects, but a closer look can reveal that his technique is more advanced.

他跳躍似於特定的派別，但是更進一步的觀看可以顯示出他的技法是更高階的。

🔑 KEY 365

-- inhospitable /ɪnh'ɑspətəbəl/ *adj.* 冷淡的、不和氣的、不親切的

● Environmental destruction has made this place **inhospitable** for migratory birds to make a temporary stay.

環境破壞已經讓這個地方不適宜遷徙的鳥類作短暫停留。

🔑 KEY 366

-- exploitation /,ɛkspl,ɔɪt'eʃən/ *n.* 開發、開采、自私的利用

● **Exploitation** of the forests is harmful to the diversity of the ecosystem.

剝削森林對於生態系統的多樣性是有害的。

🔑 KEY 367

-- exponentially /,ɛkspon'ɛnʃəli/ *adv.* 呈指數增長地

● The number of people buying tech stocks grew

exponentially in 2015, but the number plummeted significantly in the following year.

在 2015 年購買科技股的人的數量以指數性增長，但是到了次年數量有著顯著的下滑。

• KEY 368

-- immobile /ɪm'obəl/ *adj.* 不動的、不變的、固定的、靜止的

- All of a sudden, female lions remain **immobile** under the shrub, waiting for the prey to run into striking distance.

  突然之間，雌性獅子維持靜止不動待在灌木下方，等待獵物跑入攻擊距離內。

• KEY 369

-- process /pr'ɑs,ɛs/ *n.* 程序、進行、過程；*vt.* 加工、處理、對…處置、對…起訴

- The **process** of cultivating an orchid is wonderful.

  種植蘭花的過程很多采多姿。

• KEY 370

-- introduce /,ɪntrəd'us/ *vt.* 帶領、輸入、傳入；介紹；作為的開頭

- **Introducing** the new cub to other family members is such a loveable scene.

  引進新成員給其他家庭成員是多麼討人喜歡的場景。

KEY 371

-- endanger /ɛnd'endʒɚ/ vt. 危及

- The latest arrival of the new pride of lions **endangers** the current pride of lions.

  最近到來的新獅群危及到了現在獅群。

KEY 372

-- reintroduction /riɪntrəd'ʌkʃən/ n. 再次引進

- **Reintroduction** of wolves is a great way to control the population of buffalos.

  再次引進狼是控制水牛族群的很棒方式。

Unit 32 《劍 12》
Test 7 Reading Passage 2

The Intersection of Health Sciences and Geography
健康科學和地理的交集

• KEY 373 ▶ MP3 32

-- eradicate /ɪrˈædəkˌet/ *vt.* 根除、撲滅、根絕、消滅

- To **eradicate** white ants in the backyard, the landlord hires a team that uses a honey badger to eat them.
  為了根除後院的螞蟻，房東雇用了使用蜜獾來吃白蟻的團隊。

• KEY 374

-- availability /əvˌeləbˈɪləti/ *n.* 可用性、有效性；可得性【U】

- The **availability** of the traditional herb is normally ten days, but soaking it in the water can extend the preservation.
  傳統藥草的有效性通常是十天，但是將其浸泡在水中能夠延長保存期限。

• KEY 375

-- prevalent /prˈɛvələnt/ *adj.* 普遍的、流行的

- Mantises are **prevalent** in the understory of the forest, providing sufficient food resources for predators, such as chameleons.

螳螂在樹林底部普遍可見，提供給像是變色龍這樣的天敵充足的食物來源。

⚷ KEY 376

-- resistant /rɪz'ɪstənt/ *adj.* 抵抗的、反抗的

• Some animal doctors are worried that the wound of the black bear might trigger infection that is resistant to current drugs.

有些動物醫生擔憂黑熊的傷口可能會引起感染，對現今藥物有抗藥性。

⚷ KEY 377

-- massive /m'æsɪv/ *adj.* 大而重的、寬大的、宏偉的

• **Massive** rainfall makes inhabitants totally unprepared, and lots of roads are now flooding with torrents of water.

大雨讓居民全然毫無準備，而有許多道路被激流淹沒了。

⚷ KEY 378

-- industrialization /ɪnd,ʌstrɪəlɪz'eʃən/ *n.* 工業化、產業化

• **Industrialization** has created multiple jobs for local residents, but has done a lot of damage to the diversity of the forests.

工業化已經替當地居民創造了許多工作，但是也對了森林的多樣

性造成了很大的傷害。

• KEY 379

-- geography /dʒi'ɑgrəfi/ *n.* 地理；地形、地勢

* **Geography** sometimes serves as a great barrier for different prides of lions.
地勢有時候是不同獅群之間的巨大屏障。

• KEY 380

-- analyze /'ænəlˌɑɪz/ *vt.* 分析、分解

* After **analyzing** the situation, the head of the female lion initiates the attack.
在分析情勢過後，雌獅的首領發動了攻擊。

• KEY 381

-- overlay /'ovɚlˋe/ *v.* 覆蓋、重疊、覆、蓋

* Female lions use the aroma of shrubs to **overlay** the smell of the cub.
雌獅使用灌木叢的味道來覆蓋幼獸的氣味。

• KEY 382

-- discrepancy /dɪskr'ɛpənsi/ *n.* 相差、差異、差別

* The **discrepancy** between female cubs and male cubs is that female cubs stay with the pride, whereas the male cubs will eventually leave the pride.

雌性幼獸和雄性幼獸之間的差異在於雌性幼獸會待在原來的獅群裡頭，而雄性幼獸則最終回離開獅群。

• KEY 383

-- recommendation /r,ɛkəmənd'eʃən/ *n.* 推薦、介紹【U】；勸告、建議；可取之處【C】

- Even with a glowing **recommendation**, the candidate still fails to pass through the second interview.
  即使有著耀眼的推薦，候選人仍舊未通過第二次的面試。

• KEY 384

-- constitute /k'ɑnstət,ut/ *vt.* 構成、組成、任命

- A few female lions, cubs, and at least a male lion **constitute** a pride.
  幾隻雌獅、幼獸和至少一隻雄獅組成一個獅群。

Unit 33 《劍 12》
Test 7 Reading Passage 3

Music and the Emotions
音樂與情緒

• KEY 385   MP3 33

-- devoid /dɪvˈɔɪd/ *adj.* 全無的、缺乏的

• The village is entirely **devoid** of water, so villagers have to walk ten km to retrieve water from the well.
村莊完全缺乏水源，所以村民必須要走 10 公里從井中取水。

• KEY 386

-- explicit /ɪksplˈɪsət/ *adj.* 外在的、清楚的

• A glance of **explicit** appearance is still not enough to tell the freshness of the fruits.
觀看清楚的外表仍不足以判定水果的新鮮程度。

• KEY 387

-- underpinning /ˈʌndɚpˌɪnɪŋ/ *n.* 支撐、建築物下面的基礎、支柱

• The **underpinning** of the bridge is eroded by seawater, so the government has decided to cover several layers of cement onto it.

橋梁的支撐受到海水的侵蝕，所以政府已經決定要在上頭覆蓋幾層的水泥。

• KEY 388

-- pleasurable /pl'ɛʒəəbəl/ *adj.* 快樂的、愉快的、心情舒暢的

● Being in the valley is quite **pleasurable** since the scenery gives you tranquility and peace of mind.

因為風景給了你寧靜和平和的心境，因此山谷裡令人感到相當愉悅。

• KEY 389

-- straightforward /str'etf'ɔrwəd/ *adj.* 筆直的、率直的、粗獷的、明確的、簡單的、直接的

● On the first day at work, the boss is quite **straightforward** to assigned tasks, so there is not much talk about other things.

在第一天工作時，老闆相當直接的指定了工作任務，因此沒有討論太多其他的事情。

• KEY 390

-- monitor /m'ɑnətə/ *vt. vi.* 監視、監聽

● To **monitor** the spouse is considered illegal because you are violating his or her right.

監視配偶被視為是違法的，因為你侵犯了她或他的權利。

• KEY 391

-- trigger /trˈɪgɚ/ *n.* 觸發器、板機、制滑機；*vt.* 觸發、發射、引起；*vi.* 松開板柄

- To **trigger** the chemical reaction, people have to eat two different cures at the same time.
  為了激發化學反應，人們必須同時吃兩樣不同的處方。

• KEY 392

-- unresolved /ənrɪzˈɑlvd/ *adj.* 未解決的、未定義的

- The final chapter of the fiction leaves the ending **unresolved**, so readers have to wait for the next book.
  小說的最終章遺留了未決的結尾，所以讀者必須要等下一本書。

• KEY 393

-- labyrinth /lˈæbɚ,ɪnθ/ *n.* 迷宮、難解的事物、迷路

- The cellar is like a **labyrinth** so intricate in a way that the owner has to use the color label on the ground.
  地窖就像是迷宮，複雜到足以讓主人都必須要在地面上使用顏色標示。

• KEY 394

-- unpredictable /ˌʌnprɪdˈɪktəbəl/ *adj.* 不可預知的

- The **unpredictable** temper of the boss has made employees tiresome and listless.
  老闆不可預知的脾氣已經讓員工感到疲乏且無精打采。

• KEY 395

-- studious /st'udiəs/ *adj.* 愛好學問的、努力的、熱心的、勤奮的、故意的

* Being **studious** is still not enough for a disciple to pass the final test.

   勤奮仍不足以讓學徒通過最後的考試。

• KEY 396

-- flirtation /flɚt'eʃən/ *n.* 調情、挑逗、調戲

* The **flirtation** under the waterfall has turned the friendship into a torrid love affair.

   在瀑布下的調情已經使得友誼變成了火熱的愛。

Unit 34 《劍 12》
Test 8 Reading Passage 1

The History of Glass
玻璃的歷史

• KEY 397 ▶ MP3 34

-- discover /dɪsk'ʌvɚ/ *vt.* 發現、找到、暴露；*vi.* 有所發現

• Two bear cubs were thrilled that they **discovered** an abundance of honey hidden under giant trunks of trees, but soon realized that giant hornets were not that easy to tackle.

兩隻幼熊對於在巨大樹幹下發現藏匿了豐富的蜂蜜感到興奮，但馬上了解到巨型黃蜂不是那麼好應付的。

• KEY 398

-- intense /ɪnt'ɛns/ *adj.* 非常的、強烈的、緊張的、熱情的

• More than 1,000 people want the high-paying job, so the competition is extremely **intense**.

超過 1000 個人想要這份高薪工作，因此競爭是異常激烈的。

KEY 399

-- guard /gˈɑrd/ *vt.* 保衛、看守、當心；*vi.* 防止、警惕、警衛

- The tarantula exerts its one last strength to **guard** the den, but is defeated by the intruder.

  狼蛛用盡最後力氣保衛洞穴，但還是被闖入者擊敗了。

KEY 400

-- collapse /kəlˈæps/ *v.* 折疊崩潰、倒塌、虛脫；*vi.* 倒塌、崩潰、瓦解；*vt.* 使倒塌

- The burrow is collapsing, so pikas are trying to find another place to stay.

  洞穴正崩塌，所以短吻野兔正在找尋另一個棲所。

KEY 401

-- widespread /wˈɑɪdsprˈɛd/ *adj.* 廣布的、普及的、流傳寬廣的

- The **widespread** distribution of forest frogs results from increasing numbers of locusts during raining season.

  森林蛙的廣佈起因於在雨季期間日益增多的蝗蟲數量。

KEY 402

-- reputation /rˌɛpjətˈeʃən/ *n.* 名譽、聲譽、聲望、信譽

- Corn farmers have garnered a good **reputation** by cultivating delicious and juicy corn.

  玉米農夫因栽種美味且多汁的玉米而贏得好的名聲。

• KEY 403

-- craftsman /kr'æftsmən/ *n.* 工匠、技工、手藝人

- The **craftsman** has won numerous awards, but that does not measure up his earnings.

  工匠已經獲得許多獎項，但是這並沒有與他應獲取的對應收入相符。

• KEY 404

-- invaluable /ɪnv'æljəbəl/ *adj.* 無價的、價值無法衡量的

- The pearl necklace found in the trashcan proved to be **invaluable** in the long run.

  在垃圾桶裡找到的珍珠項鍊最終被現是價值連城的。

• KEY 405

-- astronomical /,æstrən'ɑmɪkəl/ *adj.* 天文學的、天文數字的、龐大的

- The divorce fee turned out to be enormous because of the violation of the prenup, and **astronomical** sums of money are needed.

  因為違反了婚前協議，離婚費用最終證實是龐大的，需要天文數字般的總額。

• KEY 406

-- levy /l'ɛvi/ *vi.* 征稅、課稅；*vt.* 徵收、發動、召集

- To maintain the operation of other divisions, the

government has to **levy** more money on the citizens this year.

為了維持其他部門的營運，政府必須在今年向市民徵收更多金錢。

KEY 407

-- numerous /n'umɚəs/ *adj.* 很多的、數目眾多的、多數的

• **Numerous** strategic moves have been put forward, but none has been adopted.

多數的策略已被提出，但是沒有一項是被採納的。

KEY 408

-- ideal /ɑɪd'il/ *adj.* 理想的、完美的、空想的、觀念的

• Looking for an **ideal** life partner can take a great deal of time.

找尋完美伴侶可能要花大量的時間。

Unit 35 《劍 12》
Test 8 Reading Passage 2

Bring Back the Big Cats
把那些大貓帶回來

• KEY 409 ▶ MP3 35

-- presume /prɪz'um/ *vt.* 假定、推測、擅自、意味著；*vi.* 擅自行動、相信

• The painting was **presumed** to have stolen by the security in the museum hundreds of years ago, but later miraculously found by the police.

這幅畫相信是在數百年前被博物館的保安人員偷走了，但是卻於之後被警方奇蹟似地找到了。

• KEY 410

-- inhabitant /ɪnh'æbətənt/ *n.* 居民、住戶、棲居的動物

• **Inhabitants** accidentally found out a miraculous herb that can be dated back to 400 years ago.

追溯到 400 年前，居民意外地發現奇蹟的藥草。

KEY 411

-- mysterious /mɪstˈɪriəs/ *adj.* 神秘的、難解的、不可思議的

- A **mysterious** disease swept over the town, and villagers could not find a cure.

  神祕的疾病掃蕩小鎮，而村民無法找到治癒的法門。

KEY 412

-- unmistakable /ˌʌnmɪstˈekəbəl/ *adj.* 不會錯的

- Wisdom of our ancestors is always **unmistakable** because that requires hundreds of years of accumulated experience.

  我們祖先的智慧總是不會錯的，因為那需要數百年的累積經驗。

KEY 413

-- restoration /rˌɛstəˈeʃən/ *n.* 恢復、歸還、復位

- **Restoration** for the museum can take more than a year, according to the news report.

  根據新聞報導指出，恢復博物館的原狀要花費超過一年的時間。

KEY 414

-- denude /dɪnˈud/ *vt.* 使裸露、剝下、剝奪

- **Plucking** rare flowers on the rock makes this place **denuded**, and recovery can take longer than predicted.

  摘岩石上罕見的花朵讓這個地方裸露，而回復期要花費比預期的時間長。

• KEY 415

-- dynamic /daɪn'æmɪk/ *adj.* 動態的、有動力的、有力的、動力的、動力、動態

- Forest squirrels are giving this place a **dynamic** appearance.
森林松鼠給予這個地方充滿生機的外貌。

• KEY 416

-- resonate /r'ɛzən,et/ *vt. vi.* （使）共鳴、（使）共振

- Other young killer whales **resonate** to the call given by adult killer whales.
年輕的殺人鯨共鳴了由其他成年殺人鯨發出的呼叫。

• KEY 417

-- commercial /kəm'ɚʃəl/ *adj.* 商業的、商用的

- The sticker is not for the **commercial** purpose, so everyone gets to download without costing a cent.
貼圖不是用於商業用途，所以每個人都能夠花不到一分錢就能下載。

• KEY 418

-- insistence /ɪns'ɪstəns/ *n.* 堅持

- **Insistence** on releasing a certain amount of captured fish has made the place more sustainable.
堅持要釋放特定量的捕獲魚使得這個地方得以永續發展。

KEY 419

-- impenetrable /ɪmpˈɛnətrəbəl/ *adj.* 不能穿過的、不可理喻的、費解的、頑固的

- In the geography of the forest, there are certain places that are **impenetrable**.

  從森林的地理來看，有特定的地方是無法穿越的。

KEY 420

-- triple /trˈɪpəl/ *vt.* 使成三倍

- The population of lobsters has **tripled** in these days, making the owner of the aquafarm ecstatic.

  龍蝦的族群已經在這幾天有三倍的成長，這使得水族農場的主人雀躍不已。

Unit 36《劍 12》
Test 8 Reading Passage 3

UK Companies Need More Effective Boards of Directors
英國公司需要更有效率的董事

• KEY 421  ▶MP3 36

-- governance /gʼʌvɚnəns/ *n.* 統轄、管理

- Corporate **governance** is not as easy as it seems because often there are multiple factors affecting every decision a CEO makes.

  公司的管理並不是看起來那樣容易,因為通常有許多因素影響著 CEO 做的每個決定。

• KEY 422

-- prolonged /prəlʼɔŋd/ *adj.* 冗長的、持久的

- **Prolonged** viewing to the smartphone screen has a detrimental effect on our eyes since our eyes cannot stand long exposure to the blue light.

  長時間觀看智慧型手機的螢幕對於我們的眼睛的影響是有害的,既然我們的眼睛無法忍受長時間曝露在藍光下。

• KEY 423

-- explanation /ˌɛksplən'eʃən/ *n.* 解釋

- Sometimes an **explanation** is needed when presenters are doing a presentation.

  有時當報告者正在做介紹時，解釋是必須的。

• KEY 424

-- scrutiny /skr'utəni/ *n.* 細看、仔細檢查

- Employees' actions are constantly under the **scrutiny** of executives, so they have to be careful about everything they do in the company.

  員工的行為不斷地受到主管的仔細檢視，所以他們必須要對於他們在公司中所做的每件事情都很小心翼翼。

• KEY 425

-- practical /pr'æktəkəl/ *adj.* 實際的、實用的

- Farmers are starting to look for a more **practical** method for pest control.

  農夫正開始找尋對於害蟲控制更實際的方法。

• KEY 426

-- restrict /rɪ'strɪkt/ *v.* 限制、約束、禁止

- Restricting the cub to get closer to places where crocodiles roam is wise.

  禁止幼獸更靠近鱷魚盤據的地方是明智的。

🔑 KEY 427

-- uncommon /ən'kɑmən/ *adj.* 不尋常的、罕見的

- It is **uncommon** to see the mating of lions in a broad daylight.

  在光天化日之下看到獅子的交配蠻不尋常的。

🔑 KEY 428

-- recruitment /rɪ'krutmənt/ *n.* 招募、補充

- **Recruitment** for a CEO sometimes requires a lengthy procedure and a great deal of time.

  聘僱 CEO 有時候需要冗長的程序與大量的時間。

🔑 KEY 429

-- remuneration /rɪmj,unɚ'reʃən/ *n.* 報酬

- After the preliminary screening and several rounds of interviews, HR managers finally discuss **remuneration** and salaries with potential recruits.

  在初次篩選和幾回合的面試後，人事經理最終和潛在的雇用人員討論了報酬和薪資。

🔑 KEY 430

-- appropriate /ə'propriət/ *adj.* 適當的、合適的

- A certain gesture is deemed **appropriate** in some countries, but is considered rude in another district.

  特定的姿勢在有些國家中被視為是合宜的，但是在另一個地區卻

被認為是無禮的。

• KEY 431

-- insatiable /ɪnsˈeʃəbəl/ *adj.* 永不滿足的；貪得無厭的

- Greedy people often have an **insatiable** urge to earn more money, and they are never going to feel satisfied.
  貪婪的人通常對於賺取更多的錢有永不滿足的慾望，而他們從不可能感到滿足。

• KEY 432

-- underperform /ˈʌndəpəˈfɔrm/ *vi.* 表現平平

- Last year, kids on the soccer team unexpectedly **underperformed**; therefore, the coach is getting increasingly nervous about the funding.
  去年，足球隊的孩子們表現平平，因此，教練對於資金補助的事情正逐漸感到緊張。

Part2

實力檢測
Vocabulary in Context

逐步強化基礎型備考者的單字理解和初階同義轉換能力，藉由這些練習漸進式到能夠獨立寫一整回劍橋雅思閱讀試題，增進信心且漸漸能在讀題和讀文章內文時產生連結，增加答題順暢度，並於時限內寫完試題。

《劍 14》 Test 1

🖉 Vocabulary in Context

❶ The turn of the actor on the horseback is considered extremely **gallant** by many cinemagoers.
gallant is in the closest meaning to this word.
A. vain   B. valid
C. valiant   D. horrific

❷ The forest flowers are toxic in a way that makes inhalers **enchanting** and hypnotic.
enchanting is in the closest meaning to this word.
A. memorizing   B. mesmerizing
C. mentoring   D. enduring

❸ Cindy is an office lady who has the **fantasy** of dating a muscular Australian fireman.
fantasy is in the closest meaning to this word.
A. problem   B. imagination
C. description   D. communication

❹ "Employee of the Month" is an award used to **extol** someone who does well in a month and will be given huge bonuses.
extol is in the closest meaning to this word.
A. inform   B. educate
C. experience   D. eulogize

❶ 男演員在馬背上的轉身被許多電影愛好者視為是極度英勇的。
gallant 的意思最接近於這個字。
A. 無效的　　　　B. 有效的
C. **勇敢的**　　　D. 可怕的

❷ 森林花朵是具有毒性的，而這種毒性能夠讓吸入者感到被誘惑且被催眠。
enchanting 的意思最接近於這個字。
A. 記憶的　　　　**B. 使人著魔的**
C. 指導　　　　　D. 永久的

❸ 辛蒂是個對與肌肉發達的澳洲消防員約會存有著幻想的上班族。
fantasy 的意思最接近於這個字。
A. 問題　　　　　**B. 想像**
C. 描述　　　　　D. 溝通

❹ 「當月最佳雇員」是個用於讚賞在一個月內表現良好者的獎勵，且會給予鉅額獎金。
extol 的意思最接近於這個字。
A. 告知　　　　　B. 教育
C. 體驗　　　　　**D. 讚美**

答案　❶ C　❷ B　❸ B　❹ D

⑤ The forest has multiple poisonous flowers, so you should be very **mindful**.

mindful is in the closest meaning to this word.

A. fragrant   B. vigilant

C. diligent   D. careless

⑥ The company has **curtailed** several benefits, such as dental and children care, due to the economic downturn.

curtailed is in the closest meaning to this word.

A. abbreviated   B. abdicated

C. admonished   D. conformed

⑦ The wicked witch has keen **perception** and mind reading, so very few people can conceal their thoughts in front of her.

perception is in the closest meaning to this word.

A. improvement   B. incentive

C. power   D. clairvoyance

⑧ Swimming in different oceans always gives Tom an **unfamiliar** feeling, and it somehow makes his skin really tactful.

unfamiliar is in the closest meaning to this word.

A. formidable   B. known

C. novel   D. famous

❺ 這個森林有多樣的毒花，因此你應該要非常注意。
mindful 的意思最接近於這個字。
A. 芬芳的　　　　B. **警覺的**
C. 勤奮的　　　　D. 粗心的

❻ 由於經濟蕭條，公司已經縮減幾項獎勵，例如牙齒和兒童照護。
curtailed 的意思最接近於這個字。
A. **刪減**　　　　B. 放棄
C. 警告　　　　　D. 遵從

❼ 邪惡的女巫有著敏銳的感知能力和讀心術，因此非常少的人能夠在她面前隱匿他們的想法。
perception 的意思最接近於這個字。
A. 改善　　　　　B. 動機
C. 力量　　　　　D. **洞察力**

❽ 在不同的海洋中游泳總是給湯姆陌生的感覺，因此他的皮膚經常非常敏感。
unfamiliar 的意思最接近於這個字。
A. 令人畏懼的　　B. 已知的
C. **新奇的**　　　D. 著名的

答案　❺ B　❻ A　❼ D　❽ C

171

9 A honey plot is a **scheme** frequently used in various circumstances, but sometimes it is futile.

scheme is in the closest meaning to this word.

A. opposition   B. discussion

C. sheer   D. machination

10 Due to the sanitation issues and other concerns, the new beverage will be strongly **opposed** by government officials.

opposed is in the closest meaning to this word.

A. objected   B. explained

C. envisioned   D. revitalized

11 Ancestors of the village had an **elaborate** notion about herbs and medicine.

elaborate is in the closest meaning to this word.

A. standard   B. crafted

C. intelligent   D. expensive

12 Meat will be evenly **distributed** to every household after the festival.

distributed is in the closest meaning to this word.

A. collapsed   B. dispersed

C. defeated   D. deliberated

❾ 美人計是在不同的情況下頻繁被使用的計謀，但是有時候卻是無效的。

scheme 的意思最接近於這個字。

A. 反對　　　　　B. 討論

C. 純粹的　　　　**D. 策劃**

❿ 由於衛生議題和其他的考量，新的飲料將受到政府官員們強烈反對。

opposed 的意思最接近於這個字。

A. 反對　　　　B. 解釋

C. 想像　　　　　D. 復甦

⓫ 村子裡的祖先們過去對於草藥和醫學有著詳盡的想法。

elaborate 的意思最接近於這個字。

A. 標準的　　　　**B. 精心編織的**

C. 智力的　　　　D. 昂貴的

⓬ 肉品將會在節慶後均分給每個家庭。

distributed 的意思最接近於這個字。

A. 瓦解　　　　　**B. 分配**

C. 擊敗　　　　　D. 深思熟慮

答案　❾ D　❿ A　⓫ B　⓬ B

⑬ Angry chameleons are quite **conspicuous** in the forests since their coloration has changed from forest green to blazing red.

conspicuous is in the closest meaning to this word.

A. prominent
B. barren
C. genuine
D. appropriate

⑭ The **glorious** chapter of his career includes his five promotions in six years.

glorious is in the closest meaning to this word.

A. considerable
B. considerate
C. splendid
D. necessary

⑮ **Abolishing** the age limit for attending the language aptitude test is still debatable.

Abolishing is in the closest meaning to this word.

A. relinquishing
B. abrogating
C. resisting
D. excavating

⑯ **Emphasizing** your strength during an interview can be a good thing.

Emphasizing is in the closest meaning to this word.

A. inferring
B. producing
C. recovering
D. accentuating

⑬ 生氣的變色龍在森林中顯得相當引人注目，因為牠們的顏色已經從森林綠轉成炙烈的紅色。

conspicuous 的意思最接近於這個字。

A. 顯眼的　　　　B. 貧瘠的

C. 真實的　　　　D. 適合的

⑭ 他榮耀的職涯篇章包含了他在六年內的五次升遷。

glorious 的意思最接近於這個字。

A. 相當多的　　　B. 體貼的

C. 輝煌的　　　　D. 必需的

⑮ 廢除參加語言性向測驗的年紀限制仍然是受爭論的。

Abolishing 的意思最接近於這個字。

A. 放棄　　　　　B. 廢除

C. 抵抗　　　　　D. 挖掘

⑯ 在面試期間，強調你的強項可能是件好事。

Emphasizing 的意思最接近於這個字。

A. 推斷　　　　　B. 產生

C. 復原　　　　　D. 強調

答案　⑬ A　⑭ C　⑮ B　⑯ D

⑰ Writing your resume in a **specifically** way can do you more good than harm.
specifically is in the closest meaning to this word.
A. typically   B. successfully
C. extraordinarily   D. concretely

⑱ Mistakes in the office can be **recurring** if the procedures are not meticulously monitored.
recurring is in the closest meaning to this word.
A. periodical   B. reducing
C. placid   D. uneasy

⑲ Writing your resume in a **succinctly** way can save HR personnel quite some time.
succinctly is in the closest meaning to this word.
A. concisely   B. mainly
C. mysteriously   D. externally

⑳ The **predisposition** of the young lady is main reason that she gets favored by the director.
predisposition is in the closest meaning to this word.
A. temper   B. temperature
C. temperament   D. depiction

⓱ 以具體地方式撰寫履歷表對於你本身來説可能是利多於弊的。
specifically 的意思最接近於這個字。
A. 典型地　　　　　B. 成功地
C. 異常地　　　　　**D. 具體地**

⓲ 如果程序沒有小心翼翼地監控的話，辦公室中的錯誤可能會是循環發生的。
recurring 的意思最接近於這個字。
A. 週期的　　　　B. 減少
C. 平靜的　　　　　D. 不安的

⓳ 以簡潔地方式撰寫你的履歷表能夠節省人事專員相當多的時間。
succinctly 的意思最接近於這個字。
A. 簡潔地　　　　B. 主要地
C. 神秘地　　　　　D. 外部地

⓴ 這位年輕女士的氣質是她受到總裁偏好的原因。
predisposition 的意思最接近於這個字。
A. 脾氣　　　　　　B. 溫度
C. 氣質　　　　　D. 描述

答案　⓱ D　⓲ A　⓳ A　⓴ C

《劍 14》 Test 2

Vocabulary in Context

❶ The **merchant** has enormous wealth due to his diplomatic relationships with several leaders in the area.
merchant is in the closest meaning to this word.
A. merchandise   B. trader
C. machine   D. wealth

❷ His **extensive** interests and hobbies make him harder to narrow down his focus and later pursuit.
extensive is in the closest meaning to this word.
A. expensive   B. expansive
C. inexpensive   D. valuable

❸ The **residence** near the tropical rainforest is a tourist spot, and is quite an important layover for multiple visitors.
residence is in the closest meaning to this word.
A. inhabitant   B. lodgment
C. location   D. collaboration

❹ In the **outskirt** of the small town, there are only a few neighborhoods, so you have to prepare enough food and drinks.
outskirt is in the closest meaning to this word.
A. collection   B. endeavor
C. suburb   D. emergence

❶ 由於他與幾位此地區的領導者有著外交關係，這位商人有巨大的財富。

merchant 的意思最接近於這個字。

A. 商品 　　　　　 B. **商人**

C. 機器 　　　　　 D. 財富

❷ 他廣泛的興趣和嗜好讓他較難於稍後的追求中窄化他的專注項目。

extensive 的意思最接近於這個字。

A. 昂貴的 　　　　 B. **廣泛的**

C. 便宜的 　　　　 D. 有價值的

❸ 在熱帶雨林附近的住宅是觀光勝地，對於許多拜訪者來說是相當重要的短暫停留處。

residence 的意思最接近於這個字。

A. 居民 　　　　　 B. **住所**

C. 位置 　　　　　 D. 合作

❹ 在小鎮的郊區，僅有幾戶人家住著，所以你必須要準備足夠的食物和飲用水。

outskirt 的意思最接近於這個字。

A. 收集 　　　　　 B. 努力

C. **郊區** 　　　　 D. 出現

答案　❶ B　❷ B　❸ B　❹ C

❺ The family of Chen **emigrated** to Australia years ago, leaving the farm uncultivated and desolate.
emigrated is in the closest meaning to this word.
A. progressed   B. migrated
C. reduced   D. improved

❻ All pupils are so excited to learn that they will be having five **excursions** in a year.
excursions is in the closest meaning to this word.
A. achievements   B. journeys
C. secrets   D. cinemas

❼ The **chairman** of the company has the brain tumor removed, but his health condition is still not good.
chairman is in the closest meaning to this word.
A. president   B. businessman
C. attendant   D. detective

❽ The **document** went abruptly missing, scaring multiple executives because it was the only copy.
document is in the closest meaning to this word.
A. performance   B. paper
C. permanence   D. temperament

❺ 陳姓一家人幾年前移居到澳洲了，遺留著未耕作和荒廢的農田。
   emigrated 的意思最接近於這個字。
   A. 進展　　　　　B. 移居
   C. 減少　　　　　D. 改善

❻ 所有小學生在得知他們在一年內將會有五次遠足感到非常興奮。
   excursions 的意思最接近於這個字。
   A. 成就　　　　　B. 旅行
   C. 秘密　　　　　D. 電影

❼ 公司的董事長已經將腦瘤移除了，但是他的健康狀況仍然不是很好。
   chairman 的意思最接近於這個字。
   A. 主席　　　　　B. 商人
   C. 出席者　　　　D. 偵探

❽ 文件突然不見嚇到眾多主管，因為那是唯一的副本。
   document 的意思最接近於這個字。
   A. 表現　　　　　B. 文件
   C. 永久　　　　　D. 性情

答案　❺ B　❻ B　❼ A　❽ B

❾ Surprisingly, the film has reached its **culmination** in an opening scene, astounding most audiences.
culmination is in the closest meaning to this word.
A. description   B. appointment
C. climax   D. passion

❿ The **gadget** is actually a plus for the selling, since most consumers find it eye-catching.
gadget is in the closest meaning to this word.
A. gourmet   B. grief
C. grace   D. instrument

⓫ College graduates often **squander** the first few years of their salaries, not knowing that money is hard-earned.
squander is in the closest meaning to this word.
A. modify   B. dissipate
C. translate   D. misunderstand

⓬ Most career advisors will suggest job-applicants that **reinvention** be the key to their future paths.
reinvention is in the closest meaning to this word.
A. abundance   B. recreation
C. opportunity   D. energy

❾ 令人感到意外的是，電影在開場就達到了高峰，讓大多數的觀眾感到驚訝。

culmination 的意思最接近於這個字。

A. 描述　　　　B. 約定

C. 高峰　　　　D. 熱情

❿ 小配件對於銷售實際上是加分的，因為大多數的消費者的目光都會被吸引。

gadget 的意思最接近於這個字。

A. 美食　　　　B. 悲傷

C. 優雅　　　　D. 機械裝置

⓫ 大學畢業生通常會浪費掉他們前幾年的薪水，沒有意識到錢是難賺的。

squander 的意思最接近於這個字。

A. 修改　　　　B. 揮霍

C. 翻譯　　　　D. 誤解

⓬ 大多數的職涯諮詢師會建議求職者再創造，這是他們未來道路的關鍵點。

reinvention 的意思最接近於這個字。

A. 豐富　　　　B. 再創造

C. 機會　　　　D. 能量

答案　❾ C　❿ D　⓫ B　⓬ B

⑬ **Reliance** on the import goods makes peddlers pretty unstable.

Reliance is in the closest meaning to this word.

A. dependence   B. development

C. convenience   D. independence

⑭ For a new recruit, **accommodating** into an unfamiliar environment is not that easy.

accommodating is in the closest meaning to this word.

A. spacious   B. annoying

C. adapting   D. undermining

⑮ Some parts of the forest have been cleared out, making this place not **habitable** for multiple birds and insects.

habitable is in the closest meaning to this word.

A. hospital   B. functional

C. international   D. hospitable

⑯ The sudden **disappearance** of over five billion bees makes thousands of acres of fruits unfertilized.

disappearance is in the closest meaning to this word.

A. approval   B. regularity

C. vanishment   D. equality

⑬ 仰賴進口商品讓小販們相當不穩定。
Reliance 的意思最接近於這個字。
A. 依賴　　　　　B. 發展
C. 便利　　　　　D. 獨立

⑭ 對於一個新的聘僱人員，適應一個不熟悉的環境並不是那麼容易的。
accommodating 的意思最接近於這個字。
A. 寬敞的　　　　B. 令人困擾的
C. 適應　　　　　D. 詆毀

⑮ 森林的有些部分已經清除了，這使得這個地方不適宜眾多的鳥類和昆蟲居住了。
habitable 的意思最接近於這個字。
A. 醫院　　　　　B. 功能的
C. 國際的　　　　D. 適宜居住的

⑯ 超過 50 億隻蜜蜂的突然消失讓數千畝的水果無法授粉。
disappearance 的意思最接近於這個字。
A. 贊同　　　　　B. 規律性
C. 消失　　　　　D. 平等

答案　⑬ A　⑭ C　⑮ D　⑯ C

⑰ The **clamor** of the night market is the main reason why he wants to relocate.
clamor is in the closest meaning to this word.
A. hubbub   B. vagueness
C. food   D. profit

⑱ Cindy is **naturally** beautiful, so she does not need any makeup.
naturally is in the closest meaning to this word.
A. descriptive   B. innately
C. national   D. equally

⑲ Swimming in a dark murky lake has given Tom a **completely** novel experience.
completely is in the closest meaning to this word.
A. gradually   B. irrelevantly
C. thoroughly   D. righteously

⑳ A **productive** land can generate more dollars than an unproductive one.
productive is in the closest meaning to this word.
A. accurate   B. prolific
C. arable   D. affordable

⑰ 夜市的喧鬧是他想要重新移居的主要原因。

clamor 的意思最接近於這個字。

A. **喧鬧聲**　　　B. 模糊

C. 食物　　　　　D. 利潤

⑱ 辛蒂天生麗質，所以她不需要任何化妝品。

naturally 的意思最接近於這個字。

A. 描述性的　　　B. **天生地**

C. 國家的　　　　D. 平等地

⑲ 在黑暗隱蔽的湖泊裡游泳給予湯姆全然的新體驗。

completely 的意思最接近於這個字。

A. 逐漸地　　　　B. 不相干地

C. **完全地**　　　D. 正直地

⑳ 一個多產的土地比起不具生產力的土地能產出更多的價值。

productive 的意思最接近於這個字。

A. 精確的　　　　B. **多產的**

C. 可耕種的　　　D. 可以負擔起的

答案　⑰ A　⑱ B　⑲ C　⑳ B

03 UNIT 《劍 14》 Test 3

✎ Vocabulary in Context

❶ The CEO talks in a very **implicit** way, not wanting to hurt anyone's feelings.
implicit is in the closest meaning to this word.
A. reserved　　　　B. flamboyant
C. positive　　　　D. negative

❷ The **phenomenon** that hornets attacking bee colonies is very common.
phenomenon is in the closest meaning to this word.
A. innovation　　　B. departure
C. novelty　　　　D. occurrence

❸ The **correspondence** has now become the proof of the treason crime, and he is now facing a life-long exclusion of the United States.
correspondence is in the closest meaning to this word.
A. similarity　　　B. difference
C. resemblance　　D. letter

❹ There are still several things for the criminal to **elucidate** so that the prosecutor will know whether he is guilty or not.
elucidate is in the closest meaning to this word.
A. expound　　　　B. solve
C. remain　　　　D. revenge

❶ 這位 CEO 以很含蓄的方式表達，不想要傷害任何人的感受。
implicit 的意思最接近於這個字。
A. 含蓄的 　　　 B. 誇張的
C. 正向的 　　　 D. 負面的

❷ 大黃蜂群攻擊蜜蜂群的現象是非常普遍的。
phenomenon 的意思最接近於這個字。
A. 創新 　　　 B. 出發
C. 新奇 　　　 D. 現象

❸ 信件現在已經成了叛國罪的證據，而他正面臨終生無法入境美國的刑期。
correspondence 的意思最接近於這個字。
A. 相似性 　　　 B. 不同
C. 相似 　　　 D. 信件

❹ 仍然有幾件事情需要釐清，這樣一來檢控官就會知道他是否有罪了。
elucidate 的意思最接近於這個字。
A. 解釋 　　　 B. 解決
C. 維持 　　　 D. 報復

答案 ❶ A ❷ D ❸ D ❹ A

⑤ The **unintelligent** snake walks into striking distance of the spider.
unintelligent is in the closest meaning to this word.
A. rudimentary   B. foolish
C. gregarious   D. euphoric

⑥ The newly recruits are given different tasks in accordance with their **competencies**.
"competencies" is in the closest meaning to this word.
A. compartments   B. abilities
C. placebos   D. scenarios

⑦ The chemical reagent is still **experimental**, so an injection can still be considered risky and destructive.
experimental is in the closest meaning to this word.
A. maudlin   B. impetuous
C. tentative   D. infallible

⑧ **Noxious** flowers can cause impairment to our breathing ability and an increase in blood pressure.
Noxious is in the closest meaning to this word.
A. inadvertent   B. euphoric
C. dexterous   D. poisonous

❺ 愚蠢的蛇，步入蜘蛛的攻擊範圍內。
unintelligent 的意思最接近於這個字。
A. 基礎的　　　　B. **愚蠢的**
C. 群居的　　　　D. 心情愉快的

❻ 新聘人員將會根據他們的能力賦予不同類型的任務。
competencies 的意思最接近於這個字。
A. 隔間　　　　　B. **能力**
C. 安慰劑　　　　D. 情節

❼ 化學試劑仍在試驗中，所以注射仍可能被視為是具有風險且具破壞性的。
experimental 的意思最接近於這個字。
A. 感情脆弱的　　B. 魯莽的
C. **試驗性的**　　D. 絕對有效的

❽ 有毒的花朵會對於我們的呼吸能力造成損害以及血壓的升高。
Noxious 的意思最接近於這個字。
A. 不經意的　　　B. 心情愉快的
C. 敏捷的　　　　D. **有毒的**

答案　❺ B　❻ B　❼ C　❽ D

❾ The **modification** of the menu has made the restaurant more popular than ever.
modification is in the closest meaning to this word.
A. alteration
B. lethargy
C. resilience
D. optimum

❿ To **deter** his son to get married with a much older woman, she sent his son away to pursue a higher learning in Europe.
deter is in the closest meaning to this word.
A. embellish
B. hinder
C. fritter
D. instigate

⓫ The **hurdle** in the first few years are tremendous, but after those years, it will become relatively effortless.
hurdle is in the closest meaning to this word.
A. corroborate
B. obstacle
C. proliferation
D. squelch

⓬ The **looming** in the desert makes it easy to believe that there is actually an oasis there.
looming is in the closest meaning to this word.
A. dormancy
B. lethargy
C. optimum
D. mirage

❾ 菜單的修改已讓餐廳比往常更為熱門。
modification 的意思最接近於這個字。
A. 修改　　　　　B. 昏睡
C. 彈性　　　　　D. 最佳效果

❿ 為了阻止他的兒子與較年長的女性結婚，她將他兒子送往歐洲更高學府求學。
deter 的意思最接近於這個字。
A. 裝飾　　　　　B. **阻礙**
C. 浪費　　　　　D. 煽動

⓫ 在頭幾年障礙很巨大，但之後就會變得不費吹灰之力。
hurdle 的意思最接近於這個字。
A. 證實　　　　　B. **障礙**
C. 激增　　　　　D. 壓扁

⓬ 沙漠中的幽影很容易讓人相信那裡實際上有綠洲的存在。
looming 的意思最接近於這個字。
A. 休眠期　　　　B. 昏睡
C. 最佳效果　　　D. **蜃景**

答案　❾ A　❿ B　⓫ B　⓬ D

⑬ That professional athletes have a better shot than amateurs is **undisputed**.
undisputed is in the closest meaning to this word.
A. noxious   B. uncontested
C. belligerent   D. tenuous

⑭ The company has **enormous** of loans and bills to pay, making banks doubting its ability to repay the money.
enormous is in the closest meaning to this word.
A. immense   B. inadvertent
C. despondent   D. dexterous

⑮ A **tiny** portion of the local residents eat beef, so the restaurants seldom have beef related dishes on the menu.
tiny is in the closest meaning to this word.
A. facetious   B. important
C. impetuous   D. slight

⑯ Certain plants **secrete** sweet and juicy juice to lure the pollinators.
secrete is in the closest meaning to this word.
A. collaborate   B. precipitate
C. excrete   D. inhibit

⑬ 專業的運動員比起業餘運動員有較佳的勝率這點是無可爭辯的。
undisputed 的意思最接近於這個字。
A. 有毒的　　　　B. **無異議的**
C. 好戰的　　　　D. 纖細的

⑭ 公司有巨大的貸款和帳單要付，這讓銀行懷疑該公司的還款能力。
enormous 的意思最接近於這個字。
A. **龐大的**　　　B. 不經意的
C. 沮喪的　　　　D. 敏捷的

⑮ 當地居民的極小部分吃牛肉，所以餐廳幾乎沒有牛肉相關的菜餚。
tiny 的意思最接近於這個字。
A. 滑稽可笑的　　B. 重要的
C. 魯莽的　　　　D. **少量的**

⑯ 特定的植物分泌甜且多汁的汁液引誘授粉者。
secrete 的意思最接近於這個字。
A. 合作　　　　　B. 加速
C. **分泌**　　　　D. 抑制

答案　⑬ B　⑭ A　⑮ D　⑯ C

⑰ Flying sea birds **infrequently** visit the cliffs, making flowers of the cliffs exceedingly rare and expensive.
infrequently is in the closest meaning to this word.
A. randomly
B. rarely
C. often
D. sometimes

⑱ The **preparation** of the dish can take more than six hours, so normally it is served during major festivals.
preparation is in the closest meaning to this word.
A. veneration
B. charlatan
C. arrangement
D. regression

⑲ Being **purposeless** in a job can be quite harmful for one's career.
purposeless is in the closest meaning to this word.
A. euphoric
B. aimless
C. infallible
D. impetuous

⑳ The farm restaurant has lost its **intrinsic** values because of the sudden pouring of cash and growing visitors.
intrinsic is in the closest meaning to this word.
A. vicarious
B. inane
C. irrevocable
D. essential

⑰ 飛翔的海鳥罕見地拜訪懸崖峭壁，讓峭壁上的花朵變得異常稀有且昂貴。

infrequently 的意思最接近於這個字。

A. 隨意地　　　　　B. **稀少地**

C. 通常　　　　　　D. 有時候

⑱ 這項菜餚的準備時間要超過六小時，所以通常在節慶期間才會出這道菜。

preparation 的意思最接近於這個字。

A. 尊敬　　　　　　B. 騙局

C. **準備工作**　　　D. 退化

⑲ 在工作中漫無目的對於一個人的職涯是有相當程度的傷害。

purposeless 的意思最接近於這個字。

A. 心情愉快的　　　B. **漫無目標的**

C. 絕對有效的　　　D. 魯莽的

⑳ 因為突然湧現的現金和日益增多的拜訪者，農場餐廳已經失去了原有的價值。

intrinsic 的意思最接近於這個字。

A. 感同身受的　　　B. 愚蠢的

C. 不可改變的　　　D. **本質的**

答案　⑰ B　⑱ C　⑲ B　⑳ D

✎ Vocabulary in Context

❶ Matsu is considered by many an **immortal** goddess protecting thousands of sea sailors.
immortal is in the closest meaning to this word.
A. reprehensible   B. reticent
C. unfading   D. impeccable

❷ To **reproduce** the same recipe is impossible since all the original manuscripts were lost hundreds of years ago.
reproduce is in the closest meaning to this word.
A. reiterate   B. relegate
C. bolster   D. duplicate

❸ There was a significant **decline** in the number of octopuses in open sea due to excessive hunting activities.
decline is in the closest meaning to this word.
A. boost   B. attrition
C. descent   D. propensity

❹ Without natural predators, the ecological balance has **deteriorated** to a certain degree, making the prairie denuded.
deteriorated is in the closest meaning to this word.
A. degenerated   B. exonerated
C. ostracized   D. reiterated

❶ 馬祖被許多人視為是不朽的女神，保護數以千計的航海員。
immortal 的意思最接近於這個字。
A. 應受指責的　　B. 沉默的
C. **不朽的**　　　D. 完美的

❷ 要複製出同樣的食譜是不可能的，因為所有的原稿都於數百年前遺失了。
reproduce 的意思最接近於這個字。
A. 重申　　　　B. 降職
C. 支持　　　　D. **複製**

❸ 在開放的海洋中，過度的捕獵活動，使得章魚數量有顯著的減少。
decline 的意思最接近於這個字。
A. 提升　　　　B. 損耗
C. **下降**　　　D. 傾向

❹ 缺乏天敵，生態的平衡已經惡化到特定的程度了，這使得大草原呈現裸露的狀態。
deteriorated 的意思最接近於這個字。
A. **衰退**　　　B.（使）免罪
C. 放逐　　　　D. 重申

答案　❶ C　❷ D　❸ C　❹ A

❺ **Complexity** of the food web is relevant to the stability of the ecosystem. **Complexity** is in the closest meaning to this word.
A. contingency   B. propensity
C. intricacy   D. liaison

❻ The police are **responding** to the event pretty seriously, since a huge blaze had engulfed a hundred people. **responding** is in the closest meaning to this word.
A. equivocating   B. depreciating
C. replying   D. relegating

❼ The **experiment** is too laborious, so many scientists have abdicated to do the continued research in this month. **experiment** is in the closest meaning to this word.
A. consistency   B. tenet
C. test   D. sham

❽ The number of lost diamonds was found under the sea floor, and the number **coincides** with the 1989 museum records of 109.
coincides is in the closest meaning to this word.
A. corresponds   B. mandates
C. exonerates   D. reinstates

⑤ 食物網的複雜度與生態系統的穩定度有關。
Complexity 的意思最接近於這個字。
A. 偶然性　　　B. 傾向
C. **複雜**　　　D. 私通

⑥ 警方對於此事件的回應相當嚴肅，因為巨大的烈焰吞噬了一百個人。
responding 的意思最接近於這個字。
A. 含糊其辭　　B. 貶低
C. **回應**　　　D. 降職

⑦ 實驗太費力了，所以在這個月許多科學家已經放棄要繼續做研究。
experiment 的意思最接近於這個字。
A. 一致性　　　B. 信條
C. **試驗**　　　D. 騙局

⑧ 遺失的鑽石數量於海洋底部找到了，而數量跟 1989 年博物館所記錄的數量 109 顆正好吻合。
coincides 的意思最接近於這個字。
A. **一致**　　　B. 命令
C. 免罪　　　　D. 使復原

答案　⑤ C　⑥ C　⑦ C　⑧ A

9 The number of people visiting museums **decreased** in 2018, but has a remarkable boost in the following year.
decreased is in the closest meaning to this word.
A. inundated   B. declined
C. circumvented   D. relegated

10 The government has decided to **extend** the compulsory education to university so that the literacy transcends some international countries.
extend is in the closest meaning to this word.
A. reiterate   B. fritter
C. lengthen   D. disseminate

11 To win the heart of consumers, **quality** of the product is very vital.
quality is in the closest meaning to this word.
A. propensity   B. vitality
C. sham   D. characteristic

12 The **movement** of the rotated machines in the farmland produces unnecessary noise.
movement is in the closest meaning to this word.
A. motion   B. misfortune
C. dormancy   D. inhibition

❾ 參觀博物館的人數於 2018 年減少，但是次年有著顯著的增加。
decreased 的意思最接近於這個字。
A. 壓倒、充滿　　B. **減少**
C. 以智取勝　　　D. 降職

❿ 政府已經決定要將義務教育延長至大學，這樣一來識字率就會超過有些國際性的國家。
extend 的意思最接近於這個字。
A. 重申　　　　　B. 浪費
C. **延長**　　　　D. 散播

⓫ 為了贏得消費者的心，產品的品質是非常重要的。
quality 的意思最接近於這個字。
A. 傾向　　　　　B. 活力
C. 騙局　　　　　D. **特性**

⓬ 在農地，轉動機械產生不必要的噪音。
movement 的意思最接近於這個字。
A. **運轉**　　　　B. 不幸
C. 冬眠　　　　　D. 抑制

答案　❾ B　❿ C　⓫ D　⓬ A

⑬ In war-torn countries, **starvation** is so unavoidable, and there is no food left, except decayed carcasses.
starvation is in the closest meaning to this word.
A. liaison
B. solace
C. misfortune
D. famine

⑭ Surprisingly, honey badgers are gallant and combative enough to **threaten** lions.
threaten is in the closest meaning to this word.
A. intimidate
B. equivocate
C. sanction
D. inundate

⑮ The result of the interview is quite **unexpected** because no one gets hired.
unexpected is in the closest meaning to this word.
A. raucous
B. oblivious
C. unanticipated
D. grievous

⑯ The huge understory basement can be quite a **reservoir** for buckets of high-quality red wine.
reservoir is in the closest meaning to this word.
A. attrition
B. depreciation
C. storehouse
D. recourse

⑬ 在飽受戰爭摧殘的國家中,飢餓是無可避免的。沒有食物留存,只剩一些已經受蝕的屍體。

starvation 的意思最接近於這個字。

A. 私通　　　　　B. 慰藉

C. 不幸　　　　**D. 飢餓**

⑭ 令人感到意外的是,蜜獾勇敢和具戰鬥性到足以威嚇獅子。

threaten 的意思最接近於這個字。

A. 脅迫　　　　B. 含糊其辭

C. 制裁　　　　　D. 充滿

⑮ 面試的結果相當地令人意外,因為沒有人被雇用。

unexpected 的意思最接近於這個字。

A. 喧鬧的　　　　B. 健忘的

C. 意料之外的　　D. 悲痛的

⑯ 巨大的底層地下室可能是相當有份量的儲存槽,存放著高品質的紅酒。

reservoir 的意思最接近於這個字。

A. 損耗　　　　　B. 貶值

C. 倉庫　　　　D. 依賴

答案 ⑬ D　⑭ A　⑮ C　⑯ C

⑰ Linda was accused of stealing the jewelry **specimen** from another company.
specimen is in the closest meaning to this word.
A. sample
B. solace
C. contingency
D. sacrifice

⑱ **Conservation** efforts for whales are needed because lots of illegal hunting are rampant these days.
Conservation is in the closest meaning to this word.
A. optimum
B. preservation
C. proliferation
D. contingency

⑲ The **collection** of wine can be laborious, but the showcase of the cellar and the wine turns out to be worthwhile and enjoyable.
collection is in the closest meaning to this word.
A. optimum
B. detriment
C. hoard
D. proliferation

⑳ A significant **reduction** in the number of people consuming in the coffee shops has led to closure of shops in the area.
reduction is in the closest meaning to this word.
A. improvement
B. decrement
C. deportation
D. discretion

⑰ 琳達被控於從另一間公司偷竊珠寶標本。
specimen 的意思最接近於這個字。
A. **標本**　　　B. 慰藉
C. 偶然性　　　D. 犧牲

⑱ 努力保護鯨魚是必須的，因為這些日子以來非法盜獵非常猖獗。
Conservation 的意思最接近於這個字。
A. 最佳效果　　B. **保存**
C. 激增　　　　D. 偶然性

⑲ 酒的收藏可能是費力的，但是展示地窖和酒終究證實是值得且令人感到愉快的。
collection 的意思最接近於這個字。
A. 最佳效果　　B. 損傷
C. **收藏品**　　D. 激增

⑳ 在咖啡店消費的人數的顯著下滑已導致這個地區的數間店的結束營業。
reduction 的意思最接近於這個字。
A. 增加　　　　B. **減少**
C. 驅逐出境　　D. 謹慎

答案　⑰ A　⑱ B　⑲ C　⑳ B

05 UNIT

《劍 13》 Test 1

Vocabulary in Context

❶ **Domestic** livestock is still not enough for local needs, so importing some is perhaps the solution.
Domestic is in the closest meaning to this word.
A. household   B. scrupulous
C. vicarious   D. sporadic

❷ To **communicate** more effectively, villagers in the valley use several gestures and signal lanterns to convey messages.
communicate is in the closest meaning to this word.
A. embellish   B. corroborate
C. regress   D. convey

❸ The **exhilarating** news came when Cindy was in the shower, and she picked up her cellphone during the shower.
exhilarating is in the closest meaning to this word.
A. thrilling   B. rudimentary
C. ostentatious   D. gregarious

❹ Tourists are eager to visit this place because all ingredients for making the dish are **authentic**.
authentic is in the closest meaning to this word.
A. inadvertent   B. genuine
C. maudlin   D. dexterous

❶ 家畜對於當地的需求仍不夠，所以進口可能是個解決之道。
Domestic 的意思最接近於這個字。
A. **家庭的**　　B. 小心的
C. 間接感受到的　D. 零星的

❷ 為了更有效地溝通，山谷中的村民們使用幾個姿勢和信號燈籠來傳達訊息。
communicate 的意思最接近於這個字。
A. 美化　　　　B. 證實
C. 退化　　　　D. **表達**

❸ 辛蒂在淋浴時收到令人感到興奮的消息，而她在淋浴期間接起了她的手機。
exhilarating 的意思最接近於這個字。
A. **令人振奮的**　B. 基礎的
C. 賣弄的　　　D. 群居的

❹ 觀光客們都很渴望拜訪這個地方因為所有製作這道菜餚的原料都很真實。
authentic 的意思最接近於這個字。
A. 不經意地　　B. **名副其實的**
C. 感情脆弱的　D. 敏捷的

答案 ❶ A ❷ D ❸ A ❹ B

❺ The merchant has a more **accurate** way to measure whether the jewelry is authentic or not.
accurate is in the closest meaning to this word.
A. charlatan   B. irrevocable
C. euphoric   D. precise

❻ Farm owners want to **highlight** the healthy food, tranquility of the valley, and striking scenery.
highlight is in the closest meaning to this word.
A. instigate   B. spotlight
C. precipitate   D. fritter

❼ Doing repetitive tasks all day makes certain types of people feel bored; thus, flexible working hours are used to reduce the **boredom**.
boredom is in the closest meaning to this word.
A. optimum   B. detriment
C. attrition   D. ennui

❽ When threatened or insecure, monkeys can be quite **agitated**.
agitated is in the closest meaning to this word.
A. impassioned   B. despondent
C. resilient   D. facetious

❺ 商人有更精確的方式來測量珠寶是否是貨真價實。
accurate 的意思最接近於這個字。
A. 騙人的　　　　B. 不可挽回的
C. 心情愉快的　　**D. 精確的**

❻ 農場主人想要強調健康食物、山谷的寧靜和引人注目的風景。
highlight 的意思最接近於這個字。
A. 煽動　　　　　**B. 使突出醒目**
C. 加速　　　　　D. 揮霍

❼ 整天都做重複性的任務讓特定類型的人感到無聊，因此，彈性的工時能用於減低無聊。
boredom 的意思最接近於這個字。
A. 最佳效果　　　B. 損傷
C. 損耗　　　　　**D. 倦怠**

❽ 當受到威脅或感到不安全感時，猴子會變得相當躁動。
agitated 的意思最接近於這個字。
A. 慷慨激昂的　B. 沮喪的
C. 有彈性的　　　D. 滑稽的

答案　❺ D　❻ B　❼ D　❽ A

9 Wasps might be **undesirable** for desert chameleons since they have stings.

undesirable is in the closest meaning to this word.

A. tantamount
B. distasteful
C. indiscriminate
D. superfluous

10 Wasps can **repeatedly** sting the target, so they always prevail in the fight.

repeatedly is in the closest meaning to this word.

A. ridiculously
B. unexpectedly
C. continually
D. convincingly

11 Whether the paralyzed tarantula gets the **pleasure** from the sting of the wasp is still debatable.

pleasure is in the closest meaning to this word.

A. contentment
B. contingency
C. attrition
D. liaison

12 Consumption of marine creatures on the top of the food chain can be quite **detrimental**.

detrimental is in the closest meaning to this word.

A. incongruous
B. raucous
C. tenacious
D. deleterious

❾ 黃蜂對於沙漠變色龍來説可能是不受歡迎的，因為他們有刺。
undesirable 的意思最接近於這個字。
A. 相稱的　　　　　　　B. **不合口味的**
C. 不分青紅皂白的　　　D. 多餘的

❿ 黃蜂能重複性地螫目標，所以他們總是在戰鬥中獲取勝利。
repeatedly 的意思最接近於這個字。
A. 荒謬地　　　　　　　B. 出乎意料之外地
C. **連續地**　　　　　　D. 令人信服地

⓫ 被癱瘓的狼蛛是否從黃蜂的叮咬中獲取快樂仍是備受爭論的。
pleasure 的意思最接近於這個字。
A. **滿足感**　　　　　　B. 偶然性
C. 損耗　　　　　　　　D. 私通

⓬ 攝食在食物鏈頂端的海洋生物可能是有害的。
detrimental 的意思最接近於這個字。
A. 不一致的　　　　　　B. 喧鬧的
C. 堅韌的　　　　　　　D. **有害的**

答案　❾ B　❿ C　⓫ A　⓬ D

PART 1 雅思精選必考字彙

PART 2 實力檢測 Vocabulary in Context

⑬ **Artificial** trees are not quite suitable for the design of this restaurant.

Artificial is in the closest meaning to this word.

A. vociferous   B. synthetic

C. fortuitous   D. impeccable

⑭ An offer from Best Airlines **enraptures** Cindy, who has been dying to get in the industry for years.

enraptures is in the closest meaning to this word.

A. inundate   B. ostracize

C. ecstasize   D. relegate

⑮ Possessing a **prestigious** degree is not a guarantee to future success.

prestigious is in the closest meaning to this word.

A. nebulous   B. distinguished

C. incongruous   D. superfluous

⑯ You cannot expect an interview to be **objective** because it is evaluated by human beings.

objective is in the closest meaning to this word.

A. fortuitous   B. impartial

C. vociferous   D. inquisitive

⑬ 人工樹對於這間餐廳的設計來説不是那麼的合適。
Artificial 的意思最接近於這個字。
A. 喧嚷的　　　　B. **合成的**
C. 吉祥的　　　　D. 完美的

⑭ 收到倍斯特航空公司的錄取通知讓辛蒂欣喜若狂，她對於進入這個產業已經期盼數年。
enraptures 的意思最接近於這個字。
A. 充滿　　　　　B. 放逐
C. **使狂喜**　　　D. 降職

⑮ 持有享譽盛名的學歷並不是未來成功的保證。
prestigious 的意思最接近於這個字。
A. 模糊的　　　　B. **著名的**
C. 不一致的　　　D. 多餘的

⑯ 你不能期待面試是客觀的因為是由人類所作的評估。
objective 的意思最接近於這個字。
A. 吉祥的　　　　B. **公正的**
C. 喧嚷的　　　　D. 好奇的

答案　⑬ B　⑭ C　⑮ B　⑯ B

⑰ The model **exhibiting** a rare temperament of being a middle-aged aristocrat is what we are looking for.
exhibiting is in the closest meaning to this word.
A. equivocating   B. relegating
C. reiterating   D. displaying

⑱ A **sophisticated** look is a downside when you are a model.
sophisticated is in the closest meaning to this word.
A. solicitous   B. experienced
C. reprehensible   D. facetious

⑲ An **irresistible** urge to eat is a great hindrance to lose weight.
irresistible is in the closest meaning to this word.
A. solicitous   B. compelling
C. bureaucratic   D. tenacious

⑳ The **enjoyment** of eating ice cream is quite transient especially when the coldness fades away.
enjoyment is in the closest meaning to this word.
A. gladness   B. contingency
C. sham   D. propensity

⑰ 模特兒所展現出罕見的中年貴族般氣質是我們所要的。
exhibiting 的意思最接近於這個字。
A. 含糊其辭　　B. 降職
C. 重申　　　　D. **展示**

⑱ 當你是個模特兒時，老練的外貌是個缺點。
sophisticated 的意思最接近於這個字。
A. 關切的　　　B. **有經驗的**
C. 應受指責的　D. 滑稽的

⑲ 無法克制吃東西的衝動是減重的一大障礙。
irresistible 的意思最接近於這個字。
A. 關切的　　　B. **難以抗拒的**
C. 官僚的　　　D. 堅韌的

⑳ 吃冰淇淋的樂趣是相當短暫的，特別是當涼感消逝的時候。
enjoyment 的意思最接近於這個字。
A. **歡喜**　　　B. 偶然性
C. 騙局　　　　D. 傾向

答案 ⑰ D　⑱ B　⑲ B　⑳ A

《劍 13》 Test 2

 Vocabulary in Context

1 Wild flowers make this place more **fragrant**, so lots of tourists love to linger there.
fragrant is in the closest meaning to this word.
A. fortuitous   B. aromatic
C. grievous   D. vociferous

2 The chef is not willing to share the key **ingredient** in public because it is a secret family recipe.
ingredient is in the closest meaning to this word.
A. tenet   B. optimum
C. gourmet   D. element

3 After kissing, the married man was unaware that the **scent** of the young lady left on his cloth.
scent is in the closest meaning to this word.
A. smell   B. detriment
C. lethargy   D. compliment

4 To **purchase** the latest smartphone, Tom has to live a really frugal lifestyle so that he will have enough cash next month.
purchase is in the closest meaning to this word.
A. instigate   B. venerate
C. regress   D. buy

❶ 野花讓這個地方更芬芳了，所以許多觀光客喜愛停留在這兒。
fragrant 的意思最接近於這個字。
A. 幸運的　　　　B. **芬香的**
C. 悲傷的　　　　D. 喧嚷的

❷ 廚師不願意在大庭廣眾下分享關鍵成分，因為這是家庭的秘密食譜。
ingredient 的意思最接近於這個字。
A. 信條　　　　　B. 最佳效果
C. 美食　　　　　D. **要素**

❸ 在親吻後，已婚男子沒有察覺到年輕女士的香氣遺留在他的衣服上了。
scent 的意思最接近於這個字。
A. **香味**　　　　B. 損傷
C. 昏睡　　　　　D. 讚美

❹ 為了購買最新型的智慧型手機，湯姆真的必須要樽節度日，這樣他下個月才能有足夠的現金。
purchase 的意思最接近於這個字。
A. 煽動　　　　　B. 尊敬
C. 退化　　　　　D. **購買**

答案　❶B　❷D　❸A　❹D

❺ Consumption of smartphones dwindled last week to only 5,000, shocking several shop owners.

Consumption is in the closest meaning to this word.

A. expenditure   B. zenith

C. proliferation   D. liaison

❻ The **ailment** is pretty mild, so the doctor does not spend so much time talking to the patient.

ailment is in the closest meaning to this word.

A. scenario   B. illness

C. exhilaration   D. connotation

❼ Transporting fruits by using livestock is not as efficient as other means of transportation.

Transporting is in the closest meaning to this word.

A. assimilating   B. delivering

C. mitigating   D. exacerbating

❽ Exorbitant fishing can damage the local ecosystem, and that requires years to recover.

Exorbitant is in the closest meaning to this word.

A. despondent   B. excessive

C. euphoric   D. maudlin

❺ 上週智慧型手機的消費減至僅 5000 隻，震驚幾間店主。
Consumption 的意思最接近於這個字。

A. **消費**　　　B. 頂點
C. 激增　　　　D. 私通

❻ 疾病相當輕微，所以醫生不用花費很多時間在跟病患談論。
ailment 的意思最接近於這個字。

A. 情節　　　　B. **疾病**
C. 興奮　　　　D. 言外之意

❼ 藉由家畜運送水果並沒有其他運輸方式那麼有效率。
Transporting 的意思最接近於這個字。

A. 理解　　　　B. **運送**
C. 減輕　　　　D. 惡化

❽ 過度捕撈會對當地生態系統造成損害，而這需要幾年來恢復。
Exorbitant 的意思最接近於這個字。

A. 沮喪　　　　B. **過高的**
C. 心情愉快的　D. 感情脆弱的

答案　❺ A　❻ B　❼ B　❽ B

⑨ **Cultivation** of the horseradish can be detrimental to the soil.
Cultivation is in the closest meaning to this word.
A. husbandry   B. connotation
C. criterion   D. placebo

⑩ The **harvest** of strawberries in this season is prolific, so the owner shares some with small animals.
harvest is in the closest meaning to this word.
A. placebo   B. reaping
C. analogy   D. atrophy

⑪ The selling of strawberries is not as **lucrative** as it used to be.
lucrative is in the closest meaning to this word.
A. profitable   B. rudimentary
C. sporadic   D. ostentatious

⑫ Females should not be the **attachment** of their husbands, and they should be financially independent.
attachment is in the closest meaning to this word.
A. panacea   B. deprivation
C. coalition   D. appendage

9 耕種山葵可能對於土壤來説是有害的。
Cultivation 的意思最接近於這個字。

A. **耕種**　　　B. 言外之意
C. 標準　　　　D. 安慰劑

10 這季草莓的收穫量是多的，所以莓果主人分享一些給小動物。
harvest 的意思最接近於這個字。

A. 安慰劑　　　B. **收獲**
C. 類比　　　　D. 萎縮

11 草莓的銷售沒有往常那樣利潤豐厚。
lucrative 的意思最接近於這個字。

A. **獲利的**　　B. 基礎的
C. 零星的　　　D. 賣弄的

12 女性不應該是她們丈夫的附屬品，而且她們應該要財務獨立。
attachment 的意思最接近於這個字。

A. 萬靈丹　　　B. 剝奪
C. 聯合　　　　D. **附屬品**

答案　**9** A　**10** B　**11** A　**12** D

⑬ The author of the famous story prefers to remain **anonymous**.

anonymous is in the closest meaning to this word.

A. vicarious
B. incognito
C. impetuous
D. euphoric

⑭ The **subtlety** of the martial arts skills can only be understood through years of deliberate practice.

subtlety is in the closest meaning to this word.

A. proficient
B. discretion
C. craftiness
D. connotation

⑮ The sudden arrival of Helen **engendered** the gossip from local residents.

engendered is in the closest meaning to this word.

A. generated
B. assimilated
C. espoused
D. extricated

⑯ **Retaining** a talented employee is arduous because he or she might have too many options.

Retaining is in the closest meaning to this word.

A. exacerbating
B. preserving
C. deploring
D. dissipating

⑬ 著名故事的作者偏好維持匿名身分。
anonymous 的意思最接近於這個字。
A. 間接感受到的　B. **隱姓埋名的**
C. 魯莽的　　　　D. 心情愉快的

⑭ 武功的精妙僅能透過數年的刻意練習來透徹理解。
subtlety 的意思最接近於這個字。
A. 精通的　　　　B. 謹慎
C. **巧妙**　　　　D. 言外之意

⑮ 海倫突然的到來引起當地人的八卦。
engendered 的意思最接近於這個字。
A. **引起**　　　　B. 理解
C. 支持　　　　　D. 使解脫

⑯ 留住有才能的員工是艱難的因為他或她可能有太多選擇。
Retaining 的意思最接近於這個字。
A. 惡化　　　　　B. **留存**
C. 悲嘆　　　　　D. 揮霍

答案　⑬ B　⑭ C　⑮ A　⑯ B

⑰ The wealth of the town rests on the **opulence** of sea creatures, such as lobsters and crabs.
opulence is in the closest meaning to this word.
A. abundance
B. connotation
C. panacea
D. analogy

⑱ Introducing a non-native species **jeopardizes** the living of local animals.
jeopardizes is in the closest meaning to this word.
A. emanates
B. extricates
C. imperils
D. espouses

⑲ Loosening the rope on the horse **unleashes** the stress it suppresses in the body.
unleashes is in the closest meaning to this word.
A. releases
B. adepts
C. adapts
D. impedes

⑳ The picturesque valley is not as **expansively** as we expected.
expansively is in the closest meaning to this word.
A. meticulously
B. maudlin
C. uncertainly
D. extensively

⑰ 小鎮的財富仰賴海洋生物的富饒，例如龍蝦和螃蟹。
opulence 的意思最接近於這個字。

A. **豐饒**   B. 言外之意
C. 萬靈丹   D. 類比

⑱ 引進外來種危害到當地動物的生活。
jeopardizes 的意思最接近於這個字。

A. 散發出   B. 使解脫
C. **危及**   D. 支持

⑲ 鬆開馬身上的繩子解放了壓抑在其身上的壓力。
unleashes 的意思最接近於這個字。

A. **釋放**   B. 擅長
C. 改編   D. 阻礙

⑳ 風景如畫的山谷沒有我們預期的那樣廣闊。
expansively 的意思最接近於這個字。

A. 小心翼翼地   B. 感情脆弱的
C. 不確定地   D. **廣泛地**

答案 ⑰ A   ⑱ C   ⑲ A   ⑳ D

《劍 13》 Test 3

 Vocabulary in Context

❶ The designer is trying to **envisage** the image of black bears that can be used in the jewelry design.
envisage is in the closest meaning to this word.
A. contemplate   B. permeate
C. forestall   D. interrogate

❷ Being **slender** has given Cindy many advantages, such as health and pursuers.
slender is in the closest meaning to this word.
A. dexterous   B. slim
C. infallible   D. maudlin

❸ To **surmount** weather conditions, explorers have decided to stay in a nearby cave, waiting for the storm to go away.
surmount is in the closest meaning to this word.
A. conquer   B. rebuke
C. redeem   D. transgress

❹ The lion cub is still too **immature** to realize the real menaces around him.
immature is in the closest meaning to this word.
A. dexterous   B. rudimentary
C. ostentatious   D. unripe

❶ 設計師正想像黑熊的圖相可能可以用於珠寶設計。
envisage 的意思最接近於這個字。
A. 思量 　　　　B. 瀰漫
C. 先發制人 　　D. 質問

❷ 維持苗條身材已經給辛蒂許多優勢，例如擁有健康和追求者。
slender 的意思最接近於這個字。
A. 敏捷的 　　　　B. 苗條的
C. 絕對有效的 　　D. 感情脆弱的

❸ 為了克服天候狀況，探索者已經決定要待在鄰近的洞穴，等待風暴遠去。
surmount 的意思最接近於這個字。
A. 克服 　　　　B. 斥責
C. 救贖 　　　　D. 違反

❹ 獅幼仍不夠成熟到能理解他周遭的真正威脅。
immature 的意思最接近於這個字。
A. 敏捷的 　　　　B. 基礎的
C. 賣弄的 　　　　D. 未成熟的

答案 ❶ A 　❷ B 　❸ A 　❹ D

5 Island lizards **indefinitely** roam on the shore, trying to escape predators and find the shelter.

indefinitely is in the closest meaning to this word.

A. unhappily　　　B. uncertainly
C. extensively　　D. inherently

6 During this time, lots of plants are starting to **germinate** and grow.

germinate is in the closest meaning to this word.

A. insinuate　　　B. sprout
C. assimilate　　　D. exacerbate

7 **Indigenous** species can sometimes be threatened by non-native species.

Indigenous is in the closest meaning to this word.

A. gregarious　　　B. dexterous
C. native　　　　　D. scrupulous

8 The advertisement **exaggerates** the therapeutic effects of lung cancer.

exaggerates is in the closest meaning to this word.

A. overstates　　　B. insinuates
C. condemns　　　D. controls

⑤ 島上蜥蜴不確定地漫遊在岸邊，試圖逃避掠食者和找到庇護所。
indefinitely 的意思最接近於這個字。

A. 不快樂地　　　　　　B. **猶豫不決地**
C. 廣泛地　　　　　　　D. 固有地

⑥ 在這個時期，許多植物正發芽和生長。
germinate 的意思最接近於這個字。

A. 暗指　　　　　　　　B. **發芽**
C. 理解　　　　　　　　D. 惡化

⑦ 本土物種有時候可能會威脅到外來物種。
Indigenous 的意思最接近於這個字。

A. 群居的　　　　　　　B. 敏捷的
C. **本土的**　　　　　　D. 小心的

⑧ 廣告誇大了肺癌的治療效果。
exaggerates 的意思最接近於這個字。

A. **誇大**　　　　　　　B. 暗指
C. 譴責　　　　　　　　D. 控制

答案　⑤ B　⑥ B　⑦ C　⑧ A

9 After a **repetitious** attempt, the octopus eventually captures an exceedingly large lobster.
repetitious is in the closest meaning to this word.
A. ubiquitous
B. repetitive
C. infallible
D. vicarious

10 Long **exposure** to the sun can make clams cooked, so they have to remain underground.
exposure is in the closest meaning to this word.
A. coalition
B. panacea
C. discretion
D. baring

11 Playing plays a **fundamental** role in how lions learn the movement, ambush, and hunting skills.
fundamental is in the closest meaning to this word.
A. reprehensible
B. elementary
C. impeccable
D. tantamount

12 Replicating the parents' way of flying, the young has a significant **boost** in his flying ability.
boost is in the closest meaning to this word.
A. development
B. increase
C. coalition
D. decrease

9 在重複性的嘗試後，章魚最終捕抓到非常大隻的龍蝦。
repetitious 的意思最接近於這個字。
A. 無處不在的　　B. **重復的**
C. 絕對有效的　　D. 間接感受到的

10 長時間曝曬在陽光下會讓牡蠣被煮熟了，所以牡蠣必須要留在地下。
exposure 的意思最接近於這個字。
A. 聯合　　　　　B. 萬靈丹
C. 謹慎　　　　　D. **裸露**

11 獅子在玩耍中學習如何律動、埋伏和狩獵技巧上扮演基礎的角色。
fundamental 的意思最接近於這個字。
A. 應受指責的　　B. **基礎的**
C. 完美的　　　　D. 相稱的

12 複製父母的飛翔方式，幼鳥在地的飛行能力上有著顯著的進步。
boost 的意思最接近於這個字。
A. 發展　　　　　B. **增加**
C. 聯合　　　　　D. 減少

答案　**9** B　**10** D　**11** B　**12** B

⑬ Female lions **speculate** that one of the missing cubs might get eaten by hyenas.
speculate is in the closest meaning to this word.
A. conjecture　　　B. communicate
C. condemn　　　　D. overturn

⑭ Desperation for a guy has **prompted** her to seek a normal cottage boy.
prompted is in the closest meaning to this word.
A. downgraded　　B. urged
C. insinuated　　　D. mitigated

⑮ **Depictions** of taboo topics have made bloggers popular.
Depictions is in the closest meaning to this word.
A. denunciation　　B. exhilaration
C. panacea　　　　D. descriptions

⑯ The chef's **unclean** way of dealing with several dishes is so unsanitary.
unclean is in the closest meaning to this word.
A. inquisitive　　　B. contaminated
C. sedentary　　　 D. clandestine

⑬ 雌性獅子推測到其中一隻失蹤的幼獸可能已經被土狼吃了。
speculate 的意思最接近於這個字。
A. **推測**　　　B. 溝通
C. 譴責　　　　D. 推翻

⑭ 急迫找到男人已經促成了她找尋普通的農村男孩。
prompted 的意思最接近於這個字。
A. 貶低　　　　B. **驅使**
C. 暗指　　　　D. 減輕

⑮ 禁忌性的話題描述已經使得部落客們火紅。
Depictions 的意思最接近於這個字。
A. 斥責　　　　B. 興奮
C. 萬靈丹　　　D. **敘述**

⑯ 廚師不乾淨的處理幾道佳餚是如此不衛生的。
unclean 的意思最接近於這個字。
A. 好期的　　　B. **受汙染的**
C. 久坐不動的　D. 神秘的

答案 ⑬ A ⑭ B ⑮ D ⑯ B

⑰ Three lions are trying to **exhaust** the strength of a small elephant.
exhaust is in the closest meaning to this word.
A. consume
B. insinuate
C. exhort
D. mitigate

⑱ The **definitive** moment for an ostrich's life depends on the kick to the abdomen of the cheetah.
definitive is in the closest meaning to this word.
A. clandestine
B. defining
C. incongruous
D. raucous

⑲ The male ostrich ultimately **exceeds** his rival winning the heart of the female ostrich.
exceeds is in the closest meaning to this word.
A. chides
B. surpasses
C. synchronizes
D. insinuates

⑳ Zebras are known for their **distinctive** stripes, whereas giraffes are noted for their long necks.
distinctive is in the closest meaning to this word.
A. tenacious
B. peculiar
C. robust
D. vociferous

⑰ 三頭獅子正試圖耗盡小象的力氣。

exhaust 的意思最接近於這個字。

A. **耗盡**　　　　B. 暗指

C. 規勸　　　　D. 減輕

⑱ 鴕鳥性命的決定性的時刻仰賴於踢在獵豹腹部的一擊。

definitive 的意思最接近於這個字。

A. 神秘的　　　　B. **決定性的**

C. 不一致的　　　D. 喧鬧的

⑲ 雄性鴕鳥最終超過了他的敵手贏得雌性鴕鳥的芳心。

exceeds 的意思最接近於這個字。

A. 嘲笑　　　　B. **優於**

C. 使同步　　　D. 暗指

⑳ 斑馬以牠們具特色的斑紋而聞名，而長頸鹿以牠們的長脖子為人所知。

distinctive 的意思最接近於這個字。

A. 堅韌的　　　　B. **獨特的**

C. 健壯的　　　　D. 喧嚷的

答案　⑰ A　⑱ B　⑲ B　⑳ B

08

U N I T

《劍 13》 Test 4

✏ Vocabulary in Context

❶ **Vessels** are sailing at an exceedingly great speed so that fishermen can catch up with the last harvest.
Vessels is in the closest meaning to this word.
A. ships   B. veins
C. placebos   D. demeanors

❷ Even though crocodiles are **dominating** the swamp and nearby river, but pythons do pose a great threat to them.
dominating is in the closest meaning to this word.
A. dissipating   B. expediting
C. insinuating   D. reigning

❸ The **misfortune** of the crocodile is to get targeted by an agile cheetah.
misfortune is in the closest meaning to this word.
A. catastrophe   B. luck
C. location   D. organ

❹ The **daunting** task is designed to frighten most newly recruits.
daunting is in the closest meaning to this word.
A. fortuitous   B. sedentary
C. reprehensible   D. formidable

❶ 船隻正以極快的速度行駛，這樣一來漁夫們就能捕獲最後一次的捕撈。
Vessels 的意思最接近於這個字。
A. **船隻**　　　B. 靜脈
C. 安慰劑　　　D. 行為

❷ 即使鱷魚在沼澤和鄰近的溪邊佔優勢，巨蟒對牠們造成很大程度的威脅。
dominating 的意思最接近於這個字。
A. 揮霍　　　　B. 促進
C. 暗指　　　　D. **占優勢**

❸ 鱷魚的不幸是被靈巧的獵豹鎖定目標。
misfortune 的意思最接近於這個字。
A. 災禍　　　　B. 幸運
C. 位置　　　　D. 器官

❹ 令人畏縮的任務是設計用來嚇唬大多數的新聘員工。
daunting 的意思最接近於這個字。
A. 吉祥的　　　B. 久坐不動的
C. 應受指責的　D. **令人畏懼的**

答案　❶A　❷D　❸A　❹D

❺ The young prince **succeeded** the throne and inherited an enormous amount of wealth.
succeeded is in the closest meaning to this word.
A. permeated   B. implemented
C. circumvented   D. acceded

❻ The CEO cannot tolerate **incompetent** employees, so layoffs are actually a common scene in the company.
incompetent is in the closest meaning to this word.
A. raucous   B. unqualified
C. prolific   D. superfluous

❼ Rainforests contain **miscellaneous** creatures, and some even have medicinal qualities.
miscellaneous is in the closest meaning to this word.
A. blended   B. inquisitive
C. nebulous   D. fortuitous

❽ Surprisingly, the price of gold **continued** to climb, eventually reaching the climax of around 1500 dollars per gram.
continued is in the closest meaning to this word.
A. predicted   B. forestalled
C. opportune   D. persisted

❺ 年輕王子繼承了王位而且繼承了巨大的財富。
succeeded 的意思最接近於這個字。
A. 瀰漫　　　　　B. 執行
C. 以智取勝　　　**D. 繼承**

❻ CEO 無法忍受沒有能力的員工，所以解雇實際上是公司中司空見慣的事。
incompetent 的意思最接近於這個字。
A. 喧鬧的　　　　**B. 不合格的**
C. 多產的　　　　D. 多餘的

❼ 熱帶雨林包含多樣的生物，而有些甚至有醫療特質。
miscellaneous 的意思最接近於這個字。
A. 繁雜的　　　　B. 好奇的
C. 模糊的　　　　D. 吉祥的

❽ 令人感到意外的是，金子的價格持續攀升，最終達到每公克大約 1500 元的高點。
continued 的意思最接近於這個字。
A. 預測　　　　　B. 先發制人
C. 適宜的　　　　**D. 持續**

答案　❺ D　❻ B　❼ A　❽ D

⑨ The **degradation** of the land makes it not profitable and valueless.
degradation is in the closest meaning to this word.
A. recourse   B. degeneration
C. retribution   D. coalition

⑩ Bacteria eventually **decompose** rotten fruits on the forest floor.
decompose is in the closest meaning to this word.
A. develop   B. disintegrate
C. circumvent   D. expedite

⑪ The cliff-like geography makes distribution of supplies rather **inconvenient** and challenging.
inconvenient is in the closest meaning to this word.
A. fastidious   B. macabre
C. auspicious   D. unfavorable

⑫ Fruits are abundant on every tree; thus, they are easily **accessible** for small insects and larger birds.
accessible is in the closest meaning to this word.
A. inquisitive   B. oblivious
C. fortuitous   D. available

⑨ 土壤的退化讓其不具利益用處且沒有價值。
degradation 的意思最接近於這個字。
A. 依賴　　　　B. **退化**
C. 報答　　　　D. 聯合

⑩ 細菌最終分解了森林底部腐敗的水果。
decompose 的意思最接近於這個字。
A. 發展　　　　B. **使分解**
C. 以智取勝　　D. 促進

⑪ 峭壁般的地理讓供給的分布相當不便且具挑戰性。
inconvenient 的意思最接近於這個字。
A. 講究的　　　B. 可怕的
C. 吉利的　　　D. **不利的**

⑫ 在每棵樹上，水果都豐碩，因此，它們更易被小型昆蟲和較大型的鳥類取用。
accessible 的意思最接近於這個字。
A. 好奇的　　　B. 健忘的
C. 吉祥的　　　D. **易於得到的**

答案　⑨ B　⑩ B　⑪ D　⑫ D

⑬ We cannot rely on **external** incentives to motivate us to learn because it will not last long.
external is in the closest meaning to this word.
A. vociferous
B. exterior
C. dexterous
D. ostentatious

⑭ Some predators are **oblivious** and cannot recall the stashed meat hidden earlier.
oblivious is in the closest meaning to this word.
A. forgetful
B. rudimentary
C. irrevocable
D. sporadic

⑮ The female impala is still **assessing** whether the male is qualified enough to mate her or not.
assessing is in the closest meaning to this word.
A. evaluating
B. chasing
C. recalling
D. memorizing

⑯ **Illiterate** kids are peculiar in the town because going to school will not cost a cent from this year.
Illiterate is in the closest meaning to this word.
A. uneducated
B. illicit
C. resilient
D. ostentatious

⑬ 我們無法仰賴外部誘因驅策我們學習,因為這樣並不持久。
external 的意思最接近於這個字。
A. 喧嚷的　　　B. **外部的**
C. 敏捷的　　　D. 賣弄的

⑭ 有些掠食者是健忘的且無法回想出稍早前儲藏的肉在哪裡。
oblivious 的意思最接近於這個字。
A. **健忘的**　　B. 基礎的
C. 不可改變的　D. 零星的

⑮ 雌性黑斑羚正評估雄性是否足以符合跟她交配的資格。
assessing 的意思最接近於這個字。
A. **評估**　　　B. 追逐
C. 回憶　　　　D. 記憶

⑯ 在小鎮裡頭,沒受過教育的小孩是罕見的,因為今年上學不會花
費到一分錢。
Illiterate 的意思最接近於這個字。
A. **沒受教育的**　B. 違法的
C. 有彈性的　　　D. 賣弄的

答案　⑬ B　⑭ A　⑮ A　⑯ A

⑰ The appearance of chameleons turning red can be the demonstration of their **displeasure**.

displeasure is in the closest meaning to this word.

A. development   B. disparity

C. atrophy   D. discontentment

⑱ The **pursuit** of wealth has turned Tom into a greedy and ruthless man.

pursuit is in the closest meaning to this word.

A. stigma   B. platitude

C. constituent   D. chase

⑲ The female tiger has a strange **sensation** towards the latest arrival.

sensation is in the closest meaning to this word.

A. competition   B. perception

C. contention   D. retribution

⑳ The male impala has found a **desirable** mate, but is get tested by her.

desirable is in the closest meaning to this word.

A. eligible   B. facetious

C. scrupulous   D. despondent

⑰ 變色龍的外表轉變成紅色可能是在展示牠們的不快。
displeasure 的意思最接近於這個字。

A. 發展　　　　B. 不同
C. 萎縮　　　　D. **不滿**

⑱ 追求財富已經使得湯姆轉變成貪婪且殘暴的男人。
pursuit 的意思最接近於這個字。

A. 汙點　　　　B. 平凡
C. 組成物　　　D. **追求**

⑲ 雌性老虎對於新來的訪客有著奇怪的感覺。
sensation 的意思最接近於這個字。

A. 競爭　　　　B. **感覺**
C. 主張　　　　D. 報答

⑳ 黑斑羚已經找到中意的伴侶，但卻要接受她的考驗。
desirable 的意思最接近於這個字。

A. **合意的**　　B. 滑稽的
C. 小心的　　　D. 沮喪的

答案 ⑰ D ⑱ D ⑲ B ⑳ A

《劍 12》 Test 5

 Vocabulary in Context

❶ Also **remarkable** is the fact that visitors are witnessing ostriches hatching their eggs in the wild Africa.
remarkable is in the closest meaning to this word.
A. prolific
B. noticeable
C. reticent
D. tenacious

❷ The particular lizard is quite **buoyant**, so it can swim nearly the surface of the water.
buoyant is in the closest meaning to this word.
A. fortuitous
B. floating
C. raucous
D. inquisitive

❸ Getting stung by malicious scorpions was an **extraordinary** experience in an African trip.
extraordinary is in the closest meaning to this word.
A. changeable
B. marvelous
C. repetitive
D. expensive

❹ Four tiger siblings are trying to **insulate** deer from its population.
insulate is in the closest meaning to this word.
A. reiterate
B. isolate
C. relegate
D. equivocate

❶ 也值得注意的是，在野地非洲，拜訪者正目睹鴕鳥孵化牠們的蛋。

remarkable 的意思最接近於這個字。

A. 多產的　　　　B. **值得注意的**

C. 沉默的　　　　D. 堅韌的

❷ 那特別的蜥蜴相當的有浮力，所以牠幾乎能游在水的表面上。

buoyant 的意思最接近於這個字。

A. 吉祥的　　　　B. **漂浮的**

C. 喧鬧的　　　　D. 好奇的

❸ 被惡毒的毒蠍螫到是這趟非洲之旅的獨特體驗。

extraordinary 的意思最接近於這個字。

A. 可改變的　　　B. **非凡的**

C. 重複的　　　　D. 昂貴的

❹ 四隻老虎兄弟姊妹正試圖將鹿從其族群中隔離出來。

insulate 的意思最接近於這個字。

A. 重申　　　　　B. **隔離**

C. 降職　　　　　D. 含糊其辭

答案　❶ B　❷ B　❸ B　❹ B

❺ The hierarchy in the pride of lions remains pretty **constant**.

constant is in the closest meaning to this word.

A. vociferous   B. reprehensible

C. unchangeable   D. inquisitive

❻ To **replicate** the experience of elder elephants, younger elephants now know how to select better meals.

replicate is in the closest meaning to this word.

A. rebuke   B. duplicate

C. repudiate   D. prognosis

❼ It is quite soothing to see all mushrooms **flourish** at the same time.

flourish is in the closest meaning to this word.

A. misconstrue   B. thrive

C. validate   D. insinuate

❽ The **remainder** of hyenas is so scared about the ensuing attack by four muscular male lions.

remainder is in the closest meaning to this word.

A. stigma   B. residue

C. horror   D. intuition

⑤ 獅群的階層維持相當的恆定。
constant 的意思最接近於這個字。
A. 喧嚷的　　　　B. 應受指責的
C. **不變的**　　　　D. 好奇的

⑥ 為了複製年長象的體驗，年輕大象現在知道要如何選擇較佳的餐點。
replicate 的意思最接近於這個字。
A. 斥責　　　　　B. **複製**
C. 駁斥　　　　　D. 預知

⑦ 看到蘑菇在同個時間繁盛是相當撫慰人心的。
flourish 的意思最接近於這個字。
A. 誤解　　　　　B. **繁盛**
C. 使有效　　　　D. 暗指

⑧ 殘餘的土狼如此懼怕四隻肌肉健壯的獅子接踵而來的攻擊。
remainder 的意思最接近於這個字。
A. 汙名　　　　　B. **剩餘物**
C. 可怕　　　　　D. 直覺

答案　⑤ C　⑥ B　⑦ B　⑧ B

9 The **monopoly** of the silver transport has led to several bloodshed.

monopoly is in the closest meaning to this word.

A. emulate　　　　　B. platitude

C. corner　　　　　D. innuendo

10 The story is so **fascinating** that kids linger there even after it is finished.

fascinating is in the closest meaning to this word.

A. nebulous　　　　B. enchanting

C. sedentary　　　　D. reprehensible

11 The young man has **amassed** enough wealth and ready to propose to his girlfriend.

amassed is in the closest meaning to this word.

A. transferred　　　B. accumulated

C. influenced　　　D. described

12 The young writer is very **productive**, writing 10 articles in only a few hours.

productive is in the closest meaning to this word.

A. nebulous　　　　B. fruitful

C. fortuitous　　　D. solicitous

❾ 銀運輸的壟斷已經導致幾個流血衝突了。
monopoly 的意思最接近於這個字。

A. 仿效　　　　B. 平凡

C. **壟斷**　　　　D. 諷刺

❿ 故事是如此吸引人以至於即使結束後，小孩仍在那流連忘返。
fascinating 的意思最接近於這個字。

A. 模糊的　　　　B. **迷人的**

C. 久坐不動的　　D. 應受指責的

⓫ 年輕男子已經累積了足夠的財富而且準備要向他女朋友求婚了。
amassed 的意思最接近於這個字。

A. 轉移　　　　B. **累積**

C. 影響　　　　D. 描述

⓬ 年輕作家非常多產，在幾小時內撰寫了 10 篇文章。
productive 的意思最接近於這個字。

A. 模糊的　　　　B. **收益好的**

C. 吉祥的　　　　D. 關切的

答案 ❾ C　❿ B　⓫ B　⓬ B

⑬ The **triumph** of outselling other companies did not last long and the figure was soon caught up in a few hours.
triumph is in the closest meaning to this word.
A. decorum
B. denunciation
C. atrophy
D. victory

⑭ **Exchanging** the role in a company is very common nowadays, so you need to be very adaptive.
Exchanging is in the closest meaning to this word.
A. deriding
B. substituting
C. incapacitating
D. transgressing

⑮ To **celebrate** the successful hunting for a giant elephant, several male lions roar for several minutes, claiming their status and power.
celebrate is in the closest meaning to this word.
A. fabricate
B. commemorate
C. communicate
D. interrogate

⑯ The **notion** of adding vegetables in a chicken soup is not novel.
notion is in the closest meaning to this word.
A. fastidiousness
B. concept
C. connotation
D. platitude

⑬ 在銷售上勝過其他公司的成功並沒有維持太久，而在幾小時內數值就被追上了。

triumph 的意思最接近於這個字。

A. 合宜　　　　　B. 斥責

C. 萎縮　　　　　**D. 勝利**

⑭ 在公司調換職務在現今是非常常見的事，所以你需要非常有適應力。

Exchanging 的意思最接近於這個字。

A. 嘲諷　　　　　**B. 調換**

C. 使無能　　　　D. 違反

⑮ 為了慶祝成功的獵捕巨型象，幾隻雄性獅子咆嘯了幾分鐘，宣示牠們的地位和權力。

celebrate 的意思最接近於這個字。

A. 捏造　　　　　**B. 慶祝**

C. 溝通　　　　　D. 質問

⑯ 添加蔬菜於雞湯裡頭的觀念並不是很新奇。

notion 的意思最接近於這個字。

A. 講究　　　　　**B. 概念**

C. 言外之意　　　D. 平凡

答案　⑬ D　⑭ B　⑮ B　⑯ B

⑰ Initially, he **intended** to file for a divorce, but did not do it, fearing that it could jeopardize his public image.
intended is in the closest meaning to this word.
A. redeemed
B. planned
C. derided
D. flouted

⑱ Farm owners has **detected** visitors might have an agenda to their cellar.
detected is in the closest meaning to this word.
A. exacerbated
B. synchronized
C. discovered
D. circumvented

⑲ To make the poison **effective**, the wine should be kept warm enough so that toxin will not distill.
effective is in the closest meaning to this word.
A. inefficient
B. efficacious
C. sufficient
D. toxic

⑳ The **principle** rests on the tide and the buoyancy of the water, so it is entirely feasible.
principle is in the closest meaning to this word.
A. discretion
B. doctrine
C. decorum
D. exhilaration

❿ 起初，他意圖提起離婚訴訟，但最終沒有這麼做，因為害怕此舉會危及他的大眾印象。
intended 的意思最接近於這個字。

A. 救贖　　　　B. **打算**
C. 嘲笑　　　　D. 嘲笑

⓱ 農場主人已經察覺到拜訪者可能對他們的地窖有不軌的意圖。
detected 的意思最接近於這個字。

A. 惡化　　　　B. 使⋯同步
C. **察覺**　　　D. 以智取勝

⓲ 為了讓此毒生效，酒應該要保存在夠溫暖的地方，這樣一來毒性就不會被蒸餾掉。
effective 的意思最接近於這個字。

A. 無效率的　　B. **靈驗的**
C. 足夠的　　　D. 有毒的

⓳ 這個原理仰賴潮汐和水的浮力，所以這樣是全然可行的。
principle 的意思最接近於這個字。

A. 謹慎　　　　B. **原理**
C. 合宜　　　　D. 興奮

答案　⓱ B　⓲ C　⓳ B　⓴ B

《劍 12》 Test 6

✏ Vocabulary in Context

❶ The **production** of watermelons cannot meet with the demand, so the price goes up.
production is in the closest meaning to this word.
A. discretion　　　　B. yield
C. contingency　　　D. consistency

❷ Closure of ten huge companies in a month has an **adverse** effect on the economy.
adverse is in the closest meaning to this word.
A. insidious　　　　B. unfavorable
C. obtrusive　　　　D. opportune

❸ His **inability** to compete with a higher offer during a bidding war led to a blame from the boss.
inability is in the closest meaning to this word.
A. demeanor　　　　B. ineptitude
C. decorum　　　　D. discretion

❹ **Sufficient** nutrients are what the children need the most.
Sufficient is in the closest meaning to this word.
A. solicitous　　　　B. adequate
C. grievous　　　　D. impeccable

❶ 西瓜的產量無法達到需求，所以價格上揚。
production 的意思最接近於這個字。

A. 謹慎　　　　B. **產量**
C. 偶然性　　　D. 一致性

❷ 在一個月內，十間大公司的倒閉對於經濟有負面的影響。
adverse 的意思最接近於這個字。

A. 陰險的　　　B. **不利的**
C. 冒失的　　　D. 適宜的

❸ 他無法在競價戰中與較高的喊價競爭導致他到老闆的責備。
inability 的意思最接近於這個字。

A. 行為　　　　B. **笨拙**
C. 合宜　　　　D. 謹慎

❹ 足夠的營養素是小孩最需要的部分。
Sufficient 的意思最接近於這個字。

A. 關切的　　　B. **足夠的**
C. 悲傷的　　　D. 完美的

答案　❶ B　❷ B　❸ B　❹ B

5 The traditional herb miraculously has **mitigated** his pain, but venom still roams in blood vessels.
mitigated is in the closest meaning to this word.
A. synchronized B. alleviated
C. fabricated D. circumvented

6 Sales bonuses have been **significantly** slashed due to the policy of the new CEO.
significantly is in the closest meaning to this word.
A. abnormally B. usually
C. remarkably D. often

7 Licking the wound of the cub is considered the comfort towards the young, **alleviating** the pain to some extent.
alleviating is in the closest meaning to this word.
A. aggravating B. solacing
C. bragging D. boasting

8 The **achievement** of earning one million dollars is highly likely for someone like Tom, who earns a lot.
achievement is in the closest meaning to this word.
A. discretion B. accomplishment
C. contingency D. demeanor

❺ 傳統的草藥已經奇蹟似地減輕他的痛，但是毒素仍舊蔓延在他的血管中。
mitigated 的意思最接近於這個字。
A. 使...同步發生　B. 減輕
C. 捏造　　　　　D. 以智取勝

❻ 由於新 CEO 的政策，銷售獎金已經遭到大幅刪減。
significantly 的意思最接近於這個字。
A. 反常地　　　　B. 通常
C. 大幅地　　　　D. 通常

❼ 舔幼獸的傷口被視為是對年輕幼獸的撫慰，減輕某種程度的痛楚。
alleviating 的意思最接近於這個字。
A. 使惡化　　　　B. 撫慰
C. 誇大　　　　　D. 誇大

❽ 賺取一百萬元的成就對於像是湯姆那樣賺很多的人來說是非常有可能的。
achievement 的意思最接近於這個字。
A. 謹慎　　　　　B. 成就
C. 偶然性　　　　D. 行為

答案　❺ B　　❻ C　　❼ B　　❽ B

9 They could not find **remains** in the coffin, deducing that someone had come here earlier and took it away.
remains is in the closest meaning to this word.
A. recourse   B. residue
C. attrition   D. propensity

10 The **advantage** of living in the house is that you do not have to pay the rent.
advantage is in the closest meaning to this word.
A. starvation   B. cooperation
C. conspiracy   D. benefit

11 The bonuses for executing this task is **substantial**, but no one volunteered in the first place.
substantial is in the closest meaning to this word.
A. clandestine   B. nebulous
C. considerable   D. sporadic

12 **Arranging** ten different manufacturers to meet in a day is difficult.
Arranging is in the closest meaning to this word.
A. synchronizing   B. methodizing
C. circumventing   D. fabricating

❾ 他們無法找到棺材裏頭的剩餘物，推論有人已經更早於他們到此並將它拿走了。

remains 的意思最接近於這個字。

A. 依賴　　　　　B. 剩餘物

C. 耗損　　　　　D. 傾向

❿ 生活在這間房子的優點是你不需要付房租。

advantage 的意思最接近於這個字。

A. 飢餓　　　　　B. 合作

C. 陰謀　　　　　D. 益處

⓫ 執行這項任務的獎金很豐碩，但是沒有人在最初的時候自告奮勇。

substantial 的意思最接近於這個字。

A. 神秘的　　　　B. 模糊的

C. 相當多的　　　D. 零星的

⓬ 一天之內要安排 10 個不同的製造商碰面是困難的。

Arranging 的意思最接近於這個字。

A. 使...同步發生　B. 按順序編排

C. 以智取勝　　　D. 捏造

答案　❾ B　❿ D　⓫ C　⓬ B

⑬ Parents all have a high **expectation** towards kids, making them stressful.
expectation is in the closest meaning to this word.
A. achievement   B. anticipation
C. consideration   D. method

⑭ **Considerable** buffalos are trying to cross the river, making the scene quite remarkable.
Considerable is in the closest meaning to this word.
A. sizeable   B. sedentary
C. solicitous   D. fortuitous

⑮ After discussing with one another, the attorney is worried that a **monumental** mistake could be made and wrong the accused.
monumental is in the closest meaning to this word.
A. advantageous   B. enormous
C. unimportant   D. trivial

⑯ Female lions are **abandoning** the weak cub because in fact only very few healthy ones will make it to adulthood.
abandoning is in the closest meaning to this word.
A. upgrading   B. discarding
C. adapting   D. fabricating

⑬ 父母對於小孩子都有很高的期望，小孩感到很大的壓力。

expectation 的意思最接近於這個字。

A. 成就　　　　　B. 期待

C. 考慮　　　　　D. 方法

⑭ 可觀的野牛正試圖穿過河，讓這個場景相當驚人。

Considerable 的意思最接近於這個字。

A. 相當多的　　　B. 久坐不動的

C. 關切的　　　　D. 吉祥的

⑮ 在彼此討論過後，律師擔憂可能會因為誤會被告，而犯下重大的錯誤。

monumental 的意思最接近於這個字。

A. 有利的　　　　B. 巨大的

C. 不重要的　　　D. 微不足道的

⑯ 雌性獅子正放棄弱的幼獸，因為實際上只有非常少的健康幼獸能活到成年。

abandoning 的意思最接近於這個字。

A. 升級　　　　　B. 丟棄

C. 改編　　　　　D. 捏造

答案　⑬ B　⑭ A　⑮ B　⑯ B

⑰ The **disadvantage** of raising dogs is that they will jump at you when you come home.
disadvantage is in the closest meaning to this word.
A. drawback   B. benefit
C. talent   D. storage

⑱ You need 80 digit numbers to **activate** the registration of the game.
activate is in the closest meaning to this word.
A. depreciate   B. support
C. fabricate   D. energize

⑲ Scientists have the **corresponding** prediction that the octopus will return to the same shelter, evading the attack by a flounder.
corresponding is in the closest meaning to this word.
A. concordant   B. imminent
C. precarious   D. perfunctory

⑳ The **compelling** move blocked attacks in different directions, making killers astounded.
compelling is in the closest meaning to this word.
A. striking   B. esoteric
C. distraught   D. plentiful

17 眷養狗的缺點是每當你回到家時，牠們會躍向你。
disadvantage 的意思最接近於這個字。
A. **缺點**　　　　B. 益處
C. 才能　　　　　D. 儲藏

18 你需要 80 個數位號碼來激活遊戲的註冊。
activate 的意思最接近於這個字。
A. 貶值　　　　　B. 支持
C. 捏造　　　　　D. **使…活躍**

19 科學家們有著一致性的預測，章魚回到相同的庇護所，以逃避比目魚的攻擊。
corresponding 的意思最接近於這個字。
A. **一致的**　　　B. 迫近的
C. 危險的　　　　D. 馬虎的

20 引人注目的動作擋下了從不同方位而來的攻擊，讓殺手們感到震驚。
compelling 的意思最接近於這個字。
A. **引人注目的**　B. 深奧的
C. 心煩意亂的　　D. 豐富的

答案　**17** A　**18** D　**19** A　**20** A

《劍 12》 Test 7

Vocabulary in Context

❶ **Uneven** distributions of tree seeds in the area make this place look like a labyrinth.
Uneven is in the closest meaning to this word.
A. esoteric   B. unequal
C. perfunctory   D. clandestine

❷ Mother polar bear and her babies are **separated** by ice floes.
separated is in the closest meaning to this word.
A. rejuvenated   B. isolated
C. ostracized   D. jeopardized

❸ His **distinct** way of using the sword somehow balances the weakness detected by foes.
distinct is in the closest meaning to this word.
A. clear   B. unique
C. equal   D. numerous

❹ His leaping **resembles** certain sects, but a closer look can reveal that his technique is more advanced.
resembles is in the closest meaning to this word.
A. facilitates   B. approximates
C. synchronizes   D. dissipates

❶ 這個地區樹的種子分布不均勻造成此地看起來像是個迷宮。

Uneven 的意思最接近於這個字。

A. 深奧的　　　　B. **不均勻的**

C. 馬虎的　　　　D. 神秘的

❷ 母北極熊和她的小孩被大浮冰分隔開來了。

separated 的意思最接近於這個字。

A. 恢復活力　　　B. **隔離**

C. 放逐　　　　　D. 危及

❸ 他獨特運劍的方式不知如何地平衡掉了敵人察覺到的劣勢。

distinct 的意思最接近於這個字。

A. 清楚的　　　　B. **獨特的**

C. 平等的　　　　D. 眾多的

❹ 他跳躍似於特定的派別，但是更進一步的觀看可以顯示出他的技法是更高階的。

resembles 的意思最接近於這個字。

A. 促進　　　　　B. **接近**

C. 使同步　　　　D. 驅散

答案　❶ B　❷ B　❸ B　❹ B

⑤ Environmental destruction has made this place **inhospitable** for migratory birds to make a temporary stay.
inhospitable is in the closest meaning to this word.
A. ambiguous   B. bleak
C. sedentary   D. gregarious

⑥ All of a sudden, female lions remain **immobile** under the shrub, waiting for the prey to run into striking distance.
immobile is in the closest meaning to this word.
A. esoteric   B. vehement
C. dormant   D. grotesque

⑦ The latest arrival of the new pride of lions **endangers** the current pride of lions.
endangers is in the closest meaning to this word.
A. lucid   B. jeopardizes
C. impedes   D. unilateral

⑧ To **eradicate** white ants in the backyard, the landlord hires a team that uses a honey badger to eat them.
eradicate is in the closest meaning to this word.
A. extricate   B. terminate
C. espouse   D. commensurate

❺ 環境破壞已經讓這個地方不適宜遷徙的鳥類作短暫停留。

inhospitable 的意思最接近於這個字。

A. 模糊的　　　B. **荒涼的**

C. 久坐不動的　D. 群居性的

❻ 突然之間，雌性獅子維持靜止不動待在灌木下方，等待獵物跑入攻擊距離內。

immobile 的意思最接近於這個字。

A. 深奧的　　　B. 熱烈的

C. **靜止的**　　D. 古怪的

❼ 最近到來的新獅群危及到了現在獅群。

endangers 的意思最接近於這個字。

A. 清楚的　　　B. **危及**

C. 阻礙　　　　D. 單邊的

❽ 為了根除後院的螞蟻，房東雇用了使用蜜獾來吃白蟻的團隊。

eradicate 的意思最接近於這個字。

A. 解救　　　　B. **滅絕**

C. 支持　　　　D. 相稱的

答案　❺ B　❻ C　❼ B　❽ B

271

9 Mantises are **prevalent** in the understory of the forest, providing sufficient food resources for predators, such as chameleons.

prevalent is in the closest meaning to this word.

A. preposterous   B. grotesque
C. esoteric   D. widespread

10 **Massive** rainfall makes inhabitants totally unprepared, and lots of roads are now flooding with torrents of water.

Massive is in the closest meaning to this word.

A. relative   B. small
C. heavy   D. oblivious

11 Female lions use the aroma of shrubs to **overlay** the smell of the cub.

overlay is in the closest meaning to this word.

A. exhort   B. cover
C. impede   D. jeopardize

12 The **discrepancy** between female cubs and male cubs is that female cubs stay with the pride, whereas the male cubs will eventually leave the pride.

discrepancy is in the closest meaning to this word.

A. dissimilarity   B. conspiracy
C. popularity   D. fame

❾ 螳螂在樹林底部普遍可見，提供給像是變色龍這樣的天敵充足的食物來源。

prevalent 的意思最接近於這個字。

A. 荒謬的　　　　B. 古怪的
C. 深奧的　　　　**D. 普遍的**

❿ 大雨讓居民全然毫無準備，而有許多道路被激流淹沒了。

Massive 的意思最接近於這個字。

A. 相對的　　　　B. 微小的
C. 重的　　　　D. 健忘的

⓫ 雌性獅子使用灌木叢的氣外覆蓋幼獸的氣味。

overlay 的意思最接近於這個字。

A. 規勸　　　　　**B. 覆蓋**
C. 阻礙　　　　　D. 危及

⓬ 雌性幼獸和雄性幼獸之間的差異在於雌性幼獸會待在原來的獅群裡頭，而雄性幼獸則最終回離開獅群。

discrepancy 的意思最接近於這個字。

A. **不同**　　　　B. 陰謀
C. 流行　　　　　D. 名聲

答案 ❾ D　❿ C　⓫ B　⓬ A

⑬ A few female lions, cubs, and at least a male lion **constitute** a pride.
constitute is in the closest meaning to this word.
A. commensurate   B. compose
C. cooperate   D. execute

⑭ The village is entirely **devoid** of water, so villagers have to walk ten km to retrieve water from the well.
devoid is in the closest meaning to this word.
A. vacant   B. sufficient
C. adequate   D. predictable

⑮ On the first day at work, the boss is quite **straightforward** to assigned tasks, so there is not much talk about other things.
straightforward is in the closest meaning to this word.
A. candid   B. indirect
C. unequivocal   D. domineering

⑯ To **trigger** the chemical reaction, people have to eat two different cures at the same time.
trigger is in the closest meaning to this word.
A. perform   B. kindle
C. beg   D. jeopardize

⑬ 幾隻雌獅、幼獸和至少一隻雄獅組成一個獅群。
constitute 的意思最接近於這個字。
A. 相稱的　　　　B. **組成**
C. 合作　　　　　D. 執行

⑭ 村莊完全缺乏水源,所以村民必須要走 10 公里從井中取水。
devoid 的意思最接近於這個字。
A. **缺乏的**　　　B. 足夠的
C. 適當的　　　　D. 可預測的

⑮ 在第一天工作時,老闆相當直接的指定了工作任務,因此沒有討論太多其他的事情。
straightforward 的意思最接近於這個字。
A. 坦然的　　　　B. 間接的
C. **毫不含糊的**　D. 跋扈的

⑯ 為了激發化學反應,人們必須同時吃兩樣不同的處方。
trigger 的意思最接近於這個字。
A. 表演　　　　　B. **燃起**
C. 乞求　　　　　D. 危及

答案　⑬ B　⑭ A　⑮ C　⑯ B

⑰ The cellar is like a **labyrinth** so intricate in a way that the owner has to use the color label on the ground.
labyrinth is in the closest meaning to this word.
A. lobby   B. location
C. lobster   D. maze

⑱ The **unpredictable** temper of the boss has made employees tiresome and listless.
Unpredictable is in the closest meaning to this word.
A. ubiquitous   B. incalculable
C. despondent   D. dexterous

⑲ Being in the valley is quite **pleasurable** since the scenery gives you tranquility and peace of mind.
pleasurable is in the closest meaning to this word.
A. tiresome   B. enjoyable
C. energetic   D. envious

⑳ Being **studious** is still not enough for a disciple to pass the final test.
studious is in the closest meaning to this word.
A. stringent   B. homogeneous
C. esoteric   D. diligent

⑰ 地窖就像是迷宮，複雜到足以讓主人都必須要在地面上使用顏色標示。

labyrinth 的意思最接近於這個字。

A. 大廳　　　　　B. 位置

C. 龍蝦　　　　　**D. 迷宮**

⑱ 老闆不可預知的脾氣已經讓員工感到疲乏且無精打采。

Unpredictable 的意思最接近於這個字。

A. 無處不在的　　**B. 不可預料的**

C. 沮喪的　　　　D. 敏捷的

⑲ 因為風景給了你寧靜和平和的心境，因此山谷裡令人感到相當愉悅。

pleasurable 的意思最接近於這個字。

A. 煩人的　　　　**B. 令人感到愉快的**

C. 充滿活力的　　D. 羨慕的

⑳ 勤奮仍不足以讓學徒功過最後的考試。

studious 的意思最接近於這個字。

A. 嚴格的　　　　B. 同質的

C. 深奧的　　　　**D. 勤奮的**

答案　⑰ D　　⑱ B　　⑲ B　　⑳ D

《劍 12》 Test 8

 Vocabulary in Context

❶ Two bear cubs were thrilled that they **discovered** an abundance of honey hidden under giant trunks of trees, but soon realized that giant hornets were not that easy to tackle.
discovered is in the closest meaning to this word.
A. disclosed   B. chided
C. conducted   D. assimilated

❷ More than 1,000 people want the high-paying job, so the competition is extremely **intense**.
intense is in the closest meaning to this word.
A. indifferent   B. acute
C. cold   D. unexpected

❸ The tarantula exerts its one last strength to **guard** the den, but is defeated by the intruder.
guard is in the closest meaning to this word.
A. battle   B. attack
C. shield   D. concoct

❹ The burrow is **collapsing**, so pikas are trying to find another place to stay.
collapsing is in the closest meaning to this word.
A. unprecedented   B. integral
C. jeopardizing   D. toppling

❶ 兩隻幼熊對於在巨大樹幹下發現藏匿了豐富的蜂蜜感到興奮，但馬上了解到巨型黃蜂不是那麼好應付的。

discovered 的意思最接近於這個字。

A. 使露出　　　　B. 責怪
C. 進行　　　　　D. 被同化

❷ 超過 1000 個人想要這份高薪工作，因此競爭是異常激烈的。

intense 的意思最接近於這個字。

A. 冷漠的　　　　B. 激烈的
C. 冷的　　　　　D. 出乎意料之外的

❸ 狼蛛用盡最後力氣保衛洞穴，但還是被闖入者擊敗了。

guard 的意思最接近於這個字。

A. 戰鬥　　　　　B. 攻擊
C. 保護　　　　　D. 捏造

❹ 洞穴正崩塌，所以短吻野兔正在找尋另一個棲所。

collapsing 的意思最接近於這個字。

A. 史無前例的　　B. 不可或缺的
C. 危及　　　　　D. 倒塌

答案　❶A　❷B　❸C　❹D

❺ Corn farmers have garnered a good **reputation** by cultivating delicious and juicy corn.
reputation is in the closest meaning to this word.
A. reputability   B. idiosyncrasy
C. conspiracy   D. rehabilitation

❻ The pearl necklace found in the trashcan proved to be **invaluable** in the long run.
invaluable is in the closest meaning to this word.
A. indifferent   B. inexpensive
C. precious   D. presumptuous

❼ **Numerous** strategic moves have been put forward, but none has been adopted.
Numerous is in the closest meaning to this word.
A. multitudinous   B. limited
C. boisterous   D. precious

❽ Looking for an **ideal** life partner can take a great deal of time.
ideal is in the closest meaning to this word.
A. flawless   B. immense
C. intimate   D. gallant

❺ 玉米農夫因栽種美味且多汁的玉米而贏得好的名聲。
reputation 的意思最接近於這個字。
A. 名譽 　　　　B. 氣質
C. 陰謀 　　　　D. 復原

❻ 在垃圾桶裡找到的珍珠項鍊最終被發現是價值連城的。
invaluable 的意思最接近於這個字。
A. 冷漠的 　　　B. 便宜的
C. 珍貴的 　　　D. 放肆的

❼ 多數的策略已被提出，但是沒有一項是被採納的。
Numerous 的意思最接近於這個字。
A. 無數的 　　　B. 有限的
C. 吵鬧的 　　　D. 珍貴的

❽ 找尋完美伴侶可能要花費大量的時間。
ideal 的意思最接近於這個字。
A. 完美的 　　　B. 龐大的
C. 親密的 　　　D. 勇敢的

答案 ❺ A ❻ C ❼ A ❽ A

⑨ A **mysterious** disease swept over the town, and villagers could not find a cure.
mysterious is in the closest meaning to this word.
A. germane
B. repugnant
C. recondite
D. magnanimous

⑩ **Restoration** for the museum can take more than a year, according to the news report.
Restoration is in the closest meaning to this word.
A. compensation
B. rehabilitation
C. manipulation
D. danger

⑪ Forest squirrels are giving this place a **dynamic** appearance.
dynamic is in the closest meaning to this word.
A. priceless
B. valuable
C. animated
D. romantic

⑫ The sticker is not for the **commercial** purpose, so everyone gets to download without costing a cent.
commercial is in the closest meaning to this word.
A. lucid
B. distraught
C. mercantile
D. perfunctory

❾ 神祕的疾病掃蕩小鎮，而村民無法找到治癒的法門。
mysterious 的意思最接近於這個字。

A. 相關的 　　　B. 令人反感的

C. **難解的** 　　D. 慷慨的

❿ 根據新聞報導指出，恢復博物館的原狀要花費超過一年的時間。
Restoration 的意思最接近於這個字。

A. 補償 　　　　B. **復原**

C. 操控 　　　　D. 危險

⓫ 森林松鼠給予這個地方充滿生機的外貌。
dynamic 的意思最接近於這個字。

A. 無價的 　　　B. 有價值的

C. **栩栩如生的** 　D. 浪漫的

⓬ 貼圖不是用於商業用途，所以每個人都能夠花不到一分錢就能下載。
commercial 的意思最接近於這個字。

A. 清楚的 　　　B. 心煩意亂的

C. **商業的** 　　D. 馬虎的

答案　❾ C　❿ B　⓫ C　⓬ C

⑬ In the geography of the forest, there are certain places that are **impenetrable**.
impenetrable is in the closest meaning to this word.
A. inaccessible   B. sordid
C. preposterous   D. notorious

⑭ Sometimes an **explanation** is needed when presenters are doing a presentation.
explanation is in the closest meaning to this word.
A. idiosyncrasy   B. clarification
C. respect   D. rehabilitation

⑮ Farmers are starting to look for a more **practical** method for pest control.
practical is in the closest meaning to this word.
A. provocative   B. pragmatic
C. presumptuous   D. grotesque

⑯ **Restricting** the cub to get closer to places where crocodiles roam is wise.
Restricting is in the closest meaning to this word.
A. reducing   B. impeding
C. inducing   D. concocting

⓭ 從森林的地理來看，有些特定的地方是無法穿越的。
impenetrable 的意思最接近於這個字。
A. 達不到的　　B. 下賤的
C. 荒謬的　　　D. 惡名遠播的

⓮ 有時當報告者正在做介紹時，解釋是必須的。
explanation 的意思最接近於這個字。
A. 氣質　　　　B. **說明**
C. 尊重　　　　D. 復原

⓯ 農夫正開始找尋對於害蟲控制更實際的方法。
practical 的意思最接近於這個字。
A. 挑撥的　　　B. **實用的**
C. 放肆的　　　D. 古怪的

⓰ 禁止幼獸更靠近鱷魚盤據的地方是明智的。
Restricting 的意思最接近於這個字。
A. 減少　　　　B. **阻礙**
C. 促進　　　　D. 捏造

答案　⓭ A　⓮ B　⓯ B　⓰ B

⑰ It is **uncommon** to see the mating of lions in a broad daylight.
uncommon is in the closest meaning to this word.
A. distraught   B. verbose
C. unusual   D. repugnant

⑱ A certain gesture is deemed **appropriate** in some countries, but is considered rude in another district.
appropriate is in the closest meaning to this word.
A. remarkable   B. regular
C. proper   D. inappropriate

⑲ Greedy people often have an **insatiable** urge to earn more money, and they are never going to feel satisfied.
insatiable is in the closest meaning to this word.
A. covetous   B. jealous
C. satisfied   D. placid

⑳ The population of lobsters has **tripled** in these days, making the owner of the aquafarm ecstatic.
tripled is in the closest meaning to this word.
A. occupied   B. quadrupled
C. habituated   D. triplicated

⑰ 在光天化日之下看到獅子的交配蠻不尋常的。
uncommon 的意思最接近於這個字。
A. 心煩意亂的　　B. 冗長的
C. **不尋常的**　　D. 令人反感的

⑱ 特定的姿勢在有些國家中被視為是合宜的，但是在另一個地區卻被認為是無禮的。
appropriate 的意思最接近於這個字。
A. 顯著的　　　　B. 規律的
C. **合適的**　　　D. 不合適的

⑲ 貪婪的人通常對於賺取更多的錢有永不滿足的慾望，而他們從不可能感到滿足。
insatiable 的意思最接近於這個字。
A. **貪婪的**　　　B. 忌妒的
C. 滿意的　　　　D. 平和的

⑳ 龍蝦的族群已經在這幾天有三倍的增長，讓水族農場的主人感到雀躍不已。
tripled 的意思最接近於這個字。
A. 佔據　　　　　B. 四倍
C. 棲息　　　　　D. **使...成三倍**

答案　⑰ C　⑱ C　⑲ A　⑳ D

13 UNIT 綜合演練 ❶

✏️ Vocabulary in Context

❶ Interviewers of the preliminary screening all **unanimously** voted against hiring candidate A, but the CEO insisted on interviewing him.
   unanimously is in the closest meaning to this word.
   A. exceedingly   B. reluctantly
   C. agreeably   D. impending

❷ He is such an intelligent baby, an infant with above average **mentality**, scoring consistently high in the IQ test.
   mentality is in the closest meaning to this word.
   A. analogy   B. intelligence
   C. antipathy   D. idiosyncrasy

❸ This bamboo dish was **originated** from China and was later modified to the new gourmet that we see today.
   originated is in the closest meaning to this word.
   A. derided   B. macabre
   C. emerged   D. concocted

❹ The government has decided to **extend** the health care to someone who is single.
   extend is in the closest meaning to this word.
   A. implement   B. concoct
   C. contract   D. lengthen

❶ 初選的面試官們一致對於 A 候選人投下了反對雇用票，但是 CEO 卻堅持要面試他。
unanimously 的意思最接近於這個字。
A. 異常地 　　　 B. 不情願地
C. 一致地 　　　 D. 迫近的

❷ 他是如此聰明的嬰孩，有著高於一般平均的智力，在 IQ 測驗上持續性地獲取高分。
mentality 的意思最接近於這個字。
A. 類比 　　　 B. 智力
C. 憎恨 　　　 D. 氣質

❸ 這道竹筍菜餚原創於中國而於稍後修改成我們今日所見到的新美食。
originated 的意思最接近於這個字。
A. 嘲諷 　　　 B. 可怕的
C. 出現 　　　 D. 捏造

❹ 政府已經決定將健康照護延伸至單身族群。
extend 的意思最接近於這個字。
A. 執行 　　　 B. 捏造
C. 收縮 　　　 D. 延長

答案　❶C　❷B　❸C　❹D

⑤ The doctor still has not told the couple the truth that the brain of their newborn baby might be **underdeveloped**.
underdeveloped is in the closest meaning to this word.
A. entire
B. developed
C. immature
D. mature

⑥ The chemical **substance** in this type of wild flowers is extremely poisonous.
substance is in the closest meaning to this word.
A. explanation
B. rehabilitation
C. idiosyncrasy
D. content

⑦ A **constructive** criticism is better than vindictive and hurtful comments.
constructive is in the closest meaning to this word.
A. provocative
B. worthwhile
C. sordid
D. notorious

⑧ Talent **retention** has been hard in the economic boom, but quite easy in the economic downturn.
retention is in the closest meaning to this word.
A. preservation
B. recruitment
C. difficulty
D. easiness

❺ 醫生仍未告知那對夫妻他們的新生小孩可能發展不完全。
underdeveloped 的意思最接近於這個字。
A. 全然的　　　　 B. 發展
C. **發育未完全的**　D. 成熟的

❻ 存在於這類型野花裡的化學物質是具有異常劇毒的。
substance 的意思最接近於這個字。
A. 解釋　　　　　 B. 復原
C. 氣質　　　　　 D. **內容物**

❼ 一則具建設性的批評比報復性和傷人的評論好得多了。
constructive 的意思最接近於這個字。
A. 挑撥的　　　　 B. **有真實價值的**
C. 下賤的　　　　 D. 惡名遠播的

❽ 在經濟繁榮時，人才留用挺困難，但於景氣蕭條時卻相當容易。
retention 的意思最接近於這個字。
A. **保留**　　　　 B. 招募
C. 困難　　　　　 D. 容易度

答案　❺ C　❻ D　❼ B　❽ A

291

9 Proponents of this theory are arguing that people are not **inherently** bad.

inherently is in the closest meaning to this word.

A. extremely   B. unanimously

C. meticulously   D. innately

10 The only horse that can be **comparable** to Guan Yu is Red Hare.

comparable is in the closest meaning to this word.

A. verbose   B. corresponding

C. lucid   D. meticulous

11 **Countless** swordsmen are hidden behind the huge rocks waiting for a surprise attack.

Countless is in the closest meaning to this word.

A. perfunctory   B. grotesque

C. innumerable   D. precarious

12 The **forefather** was wise enough to use certain blends in this dish to neutral sour flavor.

forefather is in the closest meaning to this word.

A. forecast   B. forest

C. inference   D. progenitor

❾ 這個理論的支持者正爭論著人們的天性並非與生俱來就是壞的。
inherently 的意思最接近於這個字。
A. 異常地　　　　B. 全體一致地
C. 小心翼翼地　　D. **天生地**

❿ 能夠與關羽匹配的唯一馬匹是赤兔馬。
comparable 的意思最接近於這個字。
A. 冗長的　　　　B. **相當的**
C. 清楚的　　　　D. 小心翼翼

⓫ 數之不盡的武士藏匿在巨石後方，等待突襲。
Countless 的意思最接近於這個字。
A. 馬虎的　　　　B. 古怪的
C. **無數的**　　　D. 危險的

⓬ 祖先有智慧到在這道菜餚中使用特定的混和，以中和掉酸味。
forefather 的意思最接近於這個字。
A. 預測　　　　　B. 森林
C. 推斷　　　　　D. **始祖**

答案　❾ D　❿ B　⓫ C　⓬ D

⑬ Instructions given by amateur swimmers can be unprofessional, making students feel **misguided**.
misguided is in the closest meaning to this word.
A. accused   B. insinuated
C. misdirected   D. misused

⑭ The population of crabs has been **diminishing** due to sweltering hot summer and the increasing number of octopuses.
diminishing is in the closest meaning to this word.
A. producing   B. ballooning
C. decreasing   D. increasing

⑮ A pride of lions has encountered a **bottleneck** when they are about to cross the river.
bottleneck is in the closest meaning to this word.
A. geography   B. idiosyncrasy
C. roadblock   D. antipathy

⑯ A herd of buffalos seems unified and robust, but the situation is going to have a **disorganization** by lions' ambush and surprise attack.
disorganization is in the closest meaning to this word.
A. idiosyncrasy   B. integration
C. disintegration   D. idiosyncrasy

⑬ 業餘游泳員們給予的指示可能是不專業的，這讓學生們覺得被誤導了。

misguided 的意思最接近於這個字。

A. 控告　　　　　B. 暗指

C. **受到錯誤引導**　D. 誤用

⑭ 由於悶熱的夏天和逐漸增加的章魚數量，使得螃蟹族群數量持續減少。

diminishing 的意思最接近於這個字。

A. 產生　　　　　B. 激增

C. **逐漸減少的**　　D. 增加的

⑮ 獅群在跨越河岸時面臨到瓶頸。

bottleneck 的意思最接近於這個字。

A. 地理　　　　　B. 氣質

C. **障礙物**　　　　D. 憎恨

⑯ 一群水牛似乎統一且強壯，但是在遭遇獅子的埋伏和突襲後正面臨瓦解。

disorganization 的意思最接近於這個字。

A. 氣質　　　　　B. 整合

C. **瓦解**　　　　　D. 氣質

答案　⑬ C　⑭ C　⑮ C　⑯ C

⓱ Villagers **venerate** their gods so much that anyone who is disrespectful will get punished severely.
venerate is in the closest meaning to this word.
A. antipathy   B. worship
C. abdicate   D. monopoly

⓲ Octopuses have been known for their high **intelligence**, ink, and remarkable camouflage.
intelligence is in the closest meaning to this word.
A. skill   B. warmth
C. height   D. intellect

⓳ Northern **counterparts** do not have as many medicinal components as the local ones.
counterparts is in the closest meaning to this word.
A. esoteric   B. equivalents
C. plights   D. connoisseurs

⓴ It is hard to reach a **consensus** if both parties cannot have the same goal in mind.
consensus is in the closest meaning to this word.
A. jurisdiction   B. antipathy
C. consonance   D. idiosyncrasy

⑰ 村落的人很尊敬他們的神明以至於任何對其不敬人將受到嚴懲。
venerate 的意思最接近於這個字。

A. 憎恨 　　　　　B. **崇拜**
C. 放棄 　　　　　D. 壟斷

⑱ 章魚以牠們高度的智力、墨水和驚人的偽裝聞名。
intelligence 的意思最接近於這個字。

A. 技巧 　　　　　B. 溫暖
C. 高度 　　　　　D. **智力**

⑲ 北方的聚落沒有當地聚落具有那麼多樣的醫療要件。
counterparts 的意思最接近於這個字。

A. 深奧的 　　　　B. **等價物**
C. 困境 　　　　　D. 工藝家

⑳ 如果雙方都沒有相同的目標的話，很難達成共識。
consensus 的意思最接近於這個字。

A. 審判權 　　　　B. 贈恨
C. **一致** 　　　　D. 氣質

答案　⑰ B　⑱ D　⑲ B　⑳ C

14 UNIT 綜合演練②

✏️ Vocabulary in Context

❶ To **elude** the prosecution, he dresses himself like a nun and hides himself in a remote temple.
elude is in the closest meaning to this word.
A. smooth   B. prolong
C. develop   D. evade

❷ If children need to be motivated **extrinsically**, their progress and academic success can come to a halt when there are no monetary incentives.
extrinsically is in the closest meaning to this word.
A. unassuming   B. externally
C. internally   D. nonchalant

❸ The uncultivated farmland has become fertile and restored thanks to the machine that **automatically** runs on it.
automatically is in the closest meaning to this word.
A. extremely   B. reluctantly
C. meticulously   D. unconsciously

❹ To **bolster** his confidence, the friend listed numerous companies that actually valued his specialty.
bolster is in the closest meaning to this word.
A. reduce   B. downgrade
C. strengthen   D. upgrade

❶ 為了逃避起訴,他將自己裝扮成尼姑而且藏匿在遙遠的廟宇裡。
elude 的意思最接近於這個字。

A. 使順利　　　　B. 延長
C. 發展　　　　　D. **逃避**

❷ 如果小孩需要外部因素驅策的話,他們的進步和學術成就可能在沒有金錢的誘因時就開始停滯了。
extrinsically 的意思最接近於這個字。

A. 謙虛的　　　　B. **外部地**
C. 內部地　　　　D. 冷靜的

❸ 未耕種的農地已經變得肥沃且狀態復原,多虧了農地上的機器在上頭自動地翻動著。
automatically 的意思最接近於這個字。

A. 極端地　　　　B. 勉強地
C. 小心翼翼地　　D. **無意識地**

❹ 為了增強他的自信,朋友列出了很多公司實際上珍視他的專長。
bolster 的意思最接近於這個字。

A. 減少　　　　　B. 貶低
C. **增強**　　　　D. 升級

答案 ❶D　❷B　❸D　❹C

⑤ Removing the livestock from a **dismal** farmland is actually a good thing.
dismal is in the closest meaning to this word.
A. profitable   B. bright
C. clear   D. gloomy

⑥ To **determine** who is the real killer, the jury has reached a verdict by adopting the latest evidence brought by prosecutors this morning.
determine is in the closest meaning to this word.
A. develop   B. deduct
C. decree   D. chide

⑦ The Judge has requested the defense to **examine** toxicity of different fruits and submit the report tomorrow afternoon.
examine is in the closest meaning to this word.
A. blame   B. calculate
C. scrutinize   D. dissipate

⑧ The **validity** of the test is being questioned by numerous scholars.
validity is in the closest meaning to this word.
A. decorum   B. contingency
C. effectiveness   D. atrophy

❺ 實際上，將牲畜從陰暗的農地中移除是件好事。
dismal 的意思最接近於這個字。
A. 獲利的   B. 明亮的
C. 清楚的   **D. 陰暗的**

❻ 為了決定誰是真的殺手，陪審團已經藉由採用由檢控官們今天早晨所提出的最新證據達成了判決。
determine 的意思最接近於這個字。
A. 發展   B. 扣除
C. 決定   D. 責備

❼ 法官已經要求辯方去檢視不同水果中的毒性並且於明日下午遞交報告。
examine 的意思最接近於這個字。
A. 責備   B. 計算
C. 詳細檢查   D. 揮霍

❽ 考試的有效性被許多學者們質疑。
validity 的意思最接近於這個字。
A. 合宜   B. 偶然性
C. 有效性   D. 萎縮

答案 ❺ D   ❻ C   ❼ C   ❽ C

9 While the **investigation** is still going on, the attorney has refused to talk about anything further about the case.
investigation is in the closest meaning to this word.
A. examination   B. jurisdiction
C. dilapidated   D. hatred

10 The **analysis** of the financial report remains unfinished since economists cannot seem to find an angle to start with.
analysis is in the closest meaning to this word.
A. nonchalant   B. objective
C. performance   D. anatomy

11 The **pollution** is the main reason why a lot of birds will not have a layover during their migration.
pollution is in the closest meaning to this word.
A. contamination   B. product
C. performance   D. opportunity

12 The villagers have become so hopeless and pessimistic that they eventually turn to witches to **conjure** more rainfall for the town.
conjure is in the closest meaning to this word.
A. deride   B. endanger
C. invoke   D. fabricate

❾ 既然調查仍在進行中，律師已經拒絕進一步談論任何關於這個案例。

investigation 的意思最接近於這個字。

A. 調查　　　　　B. 審判權
C. 破爛的　　　　D. 恨意

❿ 財務報告的分析仍未完成，因為經濟學者們無法找到一個可以切入的角度。

analysis 的意思最接近於這個字。

A. 冷靜的　　　　B. 目標
C. 表現　　　　　**D. 詳細分析**

⓬ 汙染是許多鳥類在他們遷徙期間沒有短暫停留的主因。

pollution 的意思最接近於這個字。

A. 污染　　　　　B. 產品
C. 表現　　　　　D. 機會

⓭ 村民們已經變得如此的希望渺茫和悲觀以至於村民們最終轉向女巫們施魔法祈求小鎮的降雨。

conjure 的意思最接近於這個字。

A. 嘲笑　　　　　B. 危及
C. 祈求　　　　　D. 捏造

答案　❾ A　❿ D　⓫ A　⓬ C

⑬ After the tenth attempt, the **simulation** of the invaluable recipe is still a huge fiasco.

simulation is in the closest meaning to this word.

A. mimicry
B. jurisdiction
C. development
D. capability

⑭ The **misperception** of the martial arts manuscripts can be deleterious to one's major organs.

misperception is in the closest meaning to this word.

A. error
B. effectiveness
C. misinterpretation
D. jurisdiction

⑮ The **entanglement** of the relationships among different characters has made audiences harder to grasp the ending.

entanglement is in the closest meaning to this word.

A. cooperation
B. involvement
C. retribution
D. punishment

⑯ The **audience** cannot wait for the next episode because the storyline is unbelievably crafted.

audience is in the closest meaning to this word.

A. landscape
B. viewer
C. citizen
D. blooper

⓭ 在第十次的嘗試後，價值連城的食譜的模仿仍舊是很大的災難。
simulation 的意思最接近於這個字。

A. 模仿　　　　　B. 審判權
C. 發展　　　　　D. 能力

⓮ 武俠原稿的錯誤解讀可能對於一個人的主要器官有害。
misperception 的意思最接近於這個字。

A. 錯誤　　　　　B. 有效
C. 誤譯　　　　　D. 審判權

⓯ 幾個角色間的感情糾纏使得觀眾更難取掌握結局。
entanglement 的意思最接近於這個字。

A. 合作　　　　　B. 纏繞
C. 報答　　　　　D. 懲罰

⓰ 觀眾無法等待下一集因為故事情節是讓人難以置信地精心編織的。
audience 的意思最接近於這個字。

A. 場景　　　　　B. 觀眾
C. 市民　　　　　D. 洋相

答案　⓭ A　⓮ C　⓯ B　⓰ B

⑰ The farm owners have **updated** pieces of machinery, so the efficiency has become unbelievably fast.
updated is in the closest meaning to this word.
A. returned
B. recovered
C. insinuated
D. renewed

⑱ **Accommodation** is still a problem for someone who cannot stand sleeping on the train.
Accommodation is in the closest meaning to this word.
A. metamorphosis
B. habitation
C. implementation
D. contingency

⑲ These types of jobs require a high level of **creativity**.
creativity is in the closest meaning to this word.
A. metamorphosis
B. originality
C. jurisdiction
D. ability

⑩ The **frustration** of not being able to hunt a chameleon leads to a kill towards another target.
frustration is in the closest meaning to this word.
A. setback
B. metamorphosis
C. triumph
D. retribution

⑰ 農場主人已經更新了數件機械，所以效率變得異常快速。
updated 的意思最接近於這個字。
A. 歸還　　　　　B. 復原
C. 暗指　　　　　**D. 更新**

⑱ 對於一些無法忍受在火車上睡覺的人來説，住宿仍舊是個問題。
Accommodation 的意思最接近於這個字。
A. 變形　　　　　**B. 住所**
C. 執行　　　　　D. 偶然性

⑲ 這些類型的工作需要高度的創意。
creativity 的意思最接近於這個字。
A. 變形　　　　　**B. 創造力**
C. 審判權　　　　D. 能力

⑳ 無法獵捕變色龍的挫折導致轉換去獵捕另一個目標。
frustration 的意思最接近於這個字。
A. 挫折　　　　B. 變形
C. 勝利　　　　　D. 報答

答案　　⑰ D　⑱ B　⑲ B　⑳ A

綜合演練 ③

❶ Corporate **governance** is not as easy as it seems because often there are multiple factors affecting every decision a CEO makes.

governance is in the closest meaning to this word.

A. intuition　　　B. auspiciousness
C. management　　D. retribution

❷ **Prolonged** viewing to the smartphone screen has a detrimental effect on our eyes since our eyes cannot stand long exposure to the blue light.

Prolonged is in the closest meaning to this word.

A. austere　　　B. persistent
C. imminent　　D. lucid

❸ After the preliminary screening and several rounds of interviews, HR managers finally discuss **remuneration** and salaries with potential recruits.

remuneration is in the closest meaning to this word.

A. auspiciousness　B. metamorphosis
C. emolument　　　D. atrophy

❹ The painting was **presumed** to have stolen by the security in the museum hundreds of years ago, but later miraculously found by the police.

presumed is in the closest meaning to this word.

A. advocated　　B. eradicated
C. assumed　　　D. encompassed

PART 1 雅思精選必考字彙

PART 2 實力檢測 Vocabulary in Context

❶ 公司的管理並不是看起來那樣容易，因為通常有許多因素影響著 CEO 做的每個決定。
governance 的意思最接近於這個字。
A. 直覺　　　　　B. 吉利
C. **管理**　　　　D. 報答

❷ 長時間觀看智慧型手機的螢幕對於我們的眼睛的影響是有害的，既然我們的眼睛無法忍受長時間曝露在藍光下。
Prolonged 的意思最接近於這個字。
A. 嚴格的　　　　B. **持久的**
C. 迫近的　　　　D. 清楚的

❸ 在初次篩選和幾回合的面試後，人事經理最終和潛在的雇用人員討論了報酬和薪資。
remuneration 的意思最接近於這個字。
A. 吉利　　　　　B. 變形
C. **酬金**　　　　D. 萎縮

❹ 這幅畫相信是在數百年前被博物館的保安人員偷走了，但是卻於之後被警方奇蹟似地找到了。
presumed 的意思最接近於這個字。
A. 主張　　　　　B. 根除
C. **假定**　　　　D. 包含

答案 ❶ C ❷ B ❸ C ❹ C

⑤ **Inhabitants** accidentally found out a miraculous herb that can be dated back to 400 years ago.
Inhabitants is in the closest meaning to this word.
A. students
B. residents
C. culmination
D. auspiciousness

⑥ Plucking rare flowers on the rock makes this place **denuded**, and recovery can take longer than predicted.
denuded is in the closest meaning to this word.
A. intact
B. encompassed
C. expropriated
D. belligerent

⑦ The divorce fee turned out to be enormous because of the violation of the prenup, and **astronomical** sums of money is needed.
astronomical is in the closest meaning to this word.
A. esoteric
B. grotesque
C. slight
D. colossal

⑧ To maintain the operation of other divisions, the government has to **levy** more money on the citizens this year.
levy is in the closest meaning to this word.
A. forecast
B. impede
C. impose
D. encompass

❺ 追溯到 400 年前，居民意外地發現奇蹟的藥草。
Inhabitants 的意思最接近於這個字。
A. 學生　　　　B. 居民
C. 達到巔峰　　D. 吉利

❻ 摘岩石上罕見的花朵讓這個地方裸露，而回復期要花費比預期的時間長。
denuded 的意思最接近於這個字。
A. 完整的　　　B. 包含
C. **剝奪**　　　D. 好戰的

❼ 因為違反了婚前協議，離婚費用最終證實是龐大的，需要天文數字般的總額。
astronomical 的意思最接近於這個字。
A. 深奧的　　　B. 古怪的
C. 輕微的　　　D. **龐大的**

❽ 為了維持其他部門的營運，政府必須在今年向市民徵收更多金錢。
levy 的意思最接近於這個字。
A. 預測　　　　B. 阻礙
C. **徵（稅）**　D. 包含

答案　❺ B　❻ C　❼ D　❽ C

9 A glance of **explicit** appearance is still not enough to tell the freshness of the fruits.
explicit is in the closest meaning to this word.
A. arduous   B. unmistakable
C. ambiguous   D. dreadful

10 To **monitor** the spouse is considered illegal because you are violating his or her right.
monitor is in the closest meaning to this word.
A. relegate   B. encompass
C. metamorphosis   D. surveillance

11 The final chapter of the fiction leaves the ending **unresolved**, so readers have to wait for the next book.
unresolved is in the closest meaning to this word.
A. grotesque   B. undefined
C. horrific   D. tenacious

12 One of the lions unexpectedly **alters** the moving direction, astounding the prey.
alters is in the closest meaning to this word.
A. controls   B. modifies
C. encompasses   D. embellishes

❾ 觀看清楚的外表仍不足以判定水果的新鮮程度。

explicit 的意思最接近於這個字。

A. 艱難的   **B. 清楚的**

C. 模糊的   D. 可怕的

❿ 監視配偶被視為是違法的，因為你侵犯了她或他的權利。

monitor 的意思最接近於這個字。

A. 降職   B. 包含

C. 變形   **D. 監視**

⓫ 小説的最終章遺留了未決的結尾，所以讀者必須要等下一本書。

unresolved 的意思最接近於這個字。

A. 古怪的   **B. 不確定的**

C. 可怕的   D. 堅韌的

⓬ 令人意想不到的是，其中一隻獅子更改了移動方向，讓獵物感到震驚。

alters 的意思最接近於這個字。

A. 控制   **B. 更改**

C. 包含   D. 裝飾

答案 ❾ B   ❿ D   ⓫ B   ⓬ B

⑬ Numerous octopuses **inhabit** the sea floor in the Pacific, making food resources rather scanty.
inhabit is in the closest meaning to this word.
A. attack
B. explore
C. occupy
D. chide

⑭ **Inaccuracy** of moving chequers on the chessboard makes them locked in an ancient tomb.
Inaccuracy is in the closest meaning to this word.
A. inability
B. metamorphosis
C. inexactness
D. auspiciousness

⑮ **Astonishing** numbers of antiques were found in an ancient tomb, making collectors thrilled.
Astonishing is in the closest meaning to this word.
A. distraught
B. verbose
C. astounding
D. presumptuous

⑯ Antitoxin **weakens** venom circulating in blood vessels.
weakens is in the closest meaning to this word.
A. lower
B. strengthen
C. debilitate
D. improve

⓭ 許多的章魚居住在太平洋的海洋底層，讓食物資源相當貧乏。
inhabit 的意思最接近於這個字。

A. 攻擊　　　　B. 探索
C. **占據**　　　D. 斥責

⓮ 不正確的移動棋盤上的棋子讓他們困在古墓裡頭。
Inaccuracy 的意思最接近於這個字。

A. 無能　　　　B. 變形
C. **不準確**　　D. 吉利

⓯ 驚人數量的古董在古墓中被發現，這讓收藏家們感到興奮。
Astonishing 的意思最接近於這個字。

A. 心煩意亂　　B. 冗長的
C. **令人震驚的**　D. 放肆的

⓰ 抗毒素弱化了循環在血管中的毒素。
weakens 的意思最接近於這個字。

A. 降低　　　　B. 增強
C. **使衰弱**　　D. 改進

答案　⓭ C　⓮ C　⓯ C　⓰ C

315

⑰ For male lions, **ceding** the ruling means losing a pride of lions.

ceding is in the closest meaning to this word.

A. controlling   B. abdicating

C. collaborating   D. squelching

⑱ HR managers are trying to find candidates who have the **attribute** of being really clever.

attribute is in the closest meaning to this word.

A. character   B. characteristic

C. talent   D. travesty

⑲ During the chase, one of the female lions is **slightly** kicked by a giraffe, but remains unharmed.

slightly is in the closest meaning to this word.

A. meticulously   B. inconsiderably

C. vehemently   D. strongly

⑳ To **reconcile** the fight between two brothers, mother bears handed in a huge slice of honey to them, footage never before seen in years.

reconcile is in the closest meaning to this word.

A. rebuke   B. harmonize

C. exhort   D. punish

⑰ 對於雄性獅子來說，放棄統治意味著失去獅群。
ceding 的意思最接近於這個字。
A. 控制　　　　B. **放棄**
C. 合作　　　　D. 壓扁

⑱ 人事經理正在找真正有聰明特質的候選人。
attribute 的意思最接近於這個字。
A. 角色　　　　B. **特性**
C. 才能　　　　D. 曲解

⑲ 在追逐期間，其中一位雌性獅子被長頸鹿輕微地踢中，但是仍維持毫髮無傷。
slightly 的意思最接近於這個字。
A. 小心翼翼地　　B. **微不足道地**
C. 激烈地　　　　D. 強烈地

⑳ 為了調停兩兄弟間的紛爭，母熊遞了一大片蜂蜜給牠們，這是幾年內未見過的視頻。
reconcile 的意思最接近於這個字。
A. 斥責　　　　B. **使和諧**
C. 規勸　　　　D. 懲罰

答案　⑰ B　⑱ B　⑲ B　⑳ B

雅思單字　附錄

精選高階字彙

placid *adj.* 寧靜的；平和的	**regression** *n.* 退化；復原
presumptuous *adj.* 放肆的；冒昧的	**vicarious** *adj.* 感同身受的
clairvoyance *n.* 洞察力	**inane** *adj.* 空虛的；愚蠢的
dissipate *v.* 使消散、揮霍	**irrevocable** *adj.* 不可挽回的
innuendo *n.* 諷刺	**reprehensible** *adj.* 應該指摘的
insidious *adj.* 陰險的；狡詐的	**relegate** *v.* 貶謫；放逐
opportune *adj.* 恰好的，適宜的	**attrition** *n.* 損耗；磨損
solicitous *adj.* 熱心的；熱切期望的	**ostracize** *v.* 放逐；排斥
emolument *n.* 薪水；津貼；酬金	**contingency** *n.* 偶然事件；可能性
recondite *adj.* 深奧的；默默無聞的	**liaison** *n.* 聯繫；私通
nonchalant *adj.* 冷靜的	**reinstate** *v.* 使恢復；使復職
hubbub *n.* 吵鬧聲；騷動	**inundate** *v.* 充滿；壓倒
unassuming *adj.* 不裝腔作勢的	**circumvent** *v.* 以智取勝
flamboyant *adj.* 浮誇的；炫耀的	**disseminate** *v.* 散播；宣傳
prognosis *n.* 預知	**raucous** *adj.* 刺耳的；喧鬧的
euphoric *adj.* 心情愉快的	**decrement** *n.* 減少、減少量
maudlin *adj.* 感情脆弱的	**vehemently** *adv.* 強烈地；熱烈地
impetuous *adj.* 魯莽的；衝動的	**ostentatious** *adj.* 炫耀的、賣弄的
tentative *adj.* 試驗性的、嘗試的	**ennui** *n.* 倦怠；無聊

精選高階字彙

infallible *adj.* 絕對可靠的；絕對有效的	**impassion** *v.* 使激動
inadvertent *adj.* 不注意的；怠慢的	**tantamount** *adj.* 同等的、相當於
dexterous *adj.* 敏捷的；靈巧的	**contentment** *n.* 滿足、知足；滿意
lethargy *n.* 昏睡；瞌睡；不活潑	**vociferous** *adj.* 喧嚷的
optimum *n.* 最適宜條件；最佳效果	**fortuitous** *adj.* 幸運的；吉祥的
embellish *v.* 美化；裝飾	**coalition** *n.* 結合、聯合
squelch *v.* 把……鎮住；壓制	**discretion** *n.* 謹慎、考慮周到
dormancy *n.* 睡眠、冬眠	**espouse** *v.* 擁護、支持
belligerent *adj.* 好戰的；好鬥的	**forestall** *v.* 先發制（人）
tenuous *adj.* 纖細的；稀薄的	**insinuate** *v.* 含沙射影地説；暗指
despondent *adj.* 沮喪的	**denunciation** *n.* 斥責；譴責；告發
facetious *adj.* 滑稽的；好開玩笑的	**clandestine** *adj.* 祕密的；暗中的
charlatan *adj.* 騙人的	**inexactness** *n.* 不正確；不精密
synchronize *v.* 同時發生	**recourse** *n.* 依靠、依賴
nebulous *adj.* 朦朧的；含糊的	**chide** *v.* 責備；責怪
retribution *n.* 報應；懲罰；報答	**perfunctory** *adj.* 敷衍的、馬虎的
macabre *adj.* 令人毛骨悚然的	**distraught** *adj.* 心煩意亂的
unfavorable *adj.* 不利的；不適宜	**esoteric** *adj.* 深奧的；難理解的
sordid *adj.* 下賤的；利慾薰心的	**grotesque** *adj.* 古怪的；怪誕的

國家圖書館出版品預行編目(CIP)資料

一次就考到雅思單字7+/ 韋爾著-- 初版. --
新北市：倍斯特, 2019.11面； 公分. --
（考用英語系列；21）
ISBN 978-986-98079-0-6（平裝附光碟）
1.國際英語語文測試系統　2.詞彙

805.189　　　　　　　　　　108016183

考用英語系列　021

一次就考到雅思寫作7⁺（附英式發音MP3）

初　　版	2019年11月	
定　　價	新台幣460元	

作　　者	韋爾
出　　版	倍斯特出版事業有限公司
發 行 人	周瑞德
電　　話	886-2-8245-6905
傳　　真	886-2-2245-6398
地　　址	23558 新北市中和區立業路83巷7號4樓
E-mail	best.books.service@gmail.com
官　　網	www.bestbookstw.com
總 編 輯	齊心瑪
封面構成	高鍾琪
內頁構成	菩薩蠻數位文化有限公司
印　　製	大亞彩色印刷製版股份有限公司

港澳地區總經銷	泛華發行代理有限公司
地　　址	香港新界將軍澳工業邨駿昌街7號2樓
電　　話	852-2798-2323
傳　　真	852-3181-3973